# NORTH ATLANTIC DRIFT

To my lovely
X May X
I love you
X Very
X X X
X X

# NORTH ATLANTIC DRIFT

Kerry O'Grady

Supported using public funding by
**ARTS COUNCIL ENGLAND**

The author is grateful for the support of Arts Council England.

ISBN-13: 978-1505570786

For Finn and Lucien

# PART ONE
## SEARCHING AND NESTING

# 1: THE SCIENTIST

Something was happening. The forces of fate had bitten me and there I was, standing in the cold outside the kitchen door under a thin March moon, waiting for Sean to appear. He took me to the island and there my story of love and loss began.

Holding my breath, I sneaked across the gravel to the tower, not breathing freely until I'd climbed the spiral stairs to the top. As long as Dad thought I was revising in my bedroom he wouldn't interfere. Up in the tower there was a good view of the road. I watched, waited and hoped that Sean would come.

Mum was away in Dublin looking after her mother, and Dad did nothing but nag me about my exams. I had to get Sean on his own, set up something that Dad couldn't interfere with. Do anything to break the monotony of my tedious life.

It was almost dark when I saw movement down by the lake. At last Sean appeared, pushing his bike along the waterside track. I hurtled down the stairs and out into the icy air. My hat kept rolling up over my ears so I held it with both hands as I ran to the lake, my heart thumping. I had to catch him before Dad came out and spoiled everything. Skidding on wet leaves, I stopped and waited until his bike wheel appeared from around a bend.

'Oh, hey.' I tried to sound as though I always strolled by the lake on winter evenings. 'I was out looking for the dogs.'

He smiled and pulled the hat up from my eyes. 'Hello, Clare.'

Earlier that day, Dad knocked on my door. He'd scanned the room for signs of studying and then spoken.

'I'm off to town if you want to come? Sean's come back to us for the season. He's heading the gannet project.'

He stooped in through the low doorway, wearing his smart jacket rather than the usual scruffy fleece, and he'd combed his awful hair. He looked almost normal and oddly cheerful. Dad had PhD students from the university every spring to help him as part of their research projects, and half of them seemed to be called Sean. He noticed my blank response.

'Sean O'Sullivan, last summer, post-grad, you can't have forgotten.'

'Sean!' I shouted. 'Brilliant.'

I smiled, remembering the party atmosphere our lonely house had taken on during the summer. Mum had laughed more and Dad had been really sociable, inviting the other students up and letting me come out to the pub with them. We hadn't smiled so much since the day Sean left.

I jumped off the bed where I'd been working hard on yet another draft of my study timetable rather than actually revising.

'Can I come, then?' I asked, slamming my laptop shut.

'Only if you're ready right now.'

'I just need to change…'

'Sorry Clare, it's now or not at all.' He stared at me with his most irritating, patronising look.

As we drove through sleety rain over the mountain road to Carran he didn't say a word but kept clearing his throat and humming. I told myself to think about something else and try to feel sorry for him. It was a good antidote to irritation.

At last we reached town and went into The Atlantic Hotel. Dad bought coffees and as we sat down next to a lovely turf fire, the door opened and a man walked in. He peeled off heavy yellow waterproofs, leaving a puddle on the floor. I was watching his dark longish hair drip rain down the neck of his grey jumper when Dad stood up, knocking our cups and making me jump. I hadn't recognised Sean with longer hair and he'd grown a short beard, too.

'You're welcome, Sean. What'll it be?' he said, shaking Sean's hand.

'Oh, Liam. Hello, thank you. A coffee would be grand.'

'And a whiskey, too?'

'Why not. I'm drenched. It's bitter out there.'

'We're by the window. You remember Clare?' Dad pointed over in my direction as he turned towards the bar. Sean nodded to me and I nodded back at him. While the barman attended to Dad, he walked over.

'Hi, Clare,' he said. 'I hardly recognised you. You're all grown up. Seems a lot can happen in a year.'

He smiled at me, which creased his face with dimples and laughter lines. Then he leaned over to kiss me on both cheeks.

'Hi,' I said, blushing. 'You're here for the gannet project?' I mumbled, stating the obvious.

'Wouldn't have missed it for the world. And how great is it that I'm back with you folks again?' He beamed and hugged me. 'You're looking so like your gorgeous mother. I suppose you'll be what... eighteen now?'

'Um, I'm seventeen, nearly eighteen,' I croaked.

'So, Clare, will you be helping us on the project?'

'No,' I said. Seeing his smile fade, I quickly dissembled. 'I'd like to, though. I help Dad a bit sometimes. If there's anything...'

Sean looked at me thoughtfully. 'I seem to remember you were doing IT at school and you know your way around a computer.'

'Yeah, I suppose, and I've got Mum's old laptop now.'

'I remember you were good at numbers. There'll be a lot of collating to do with the project. I'm sure we can find you a job.'

He smiled at me and I wished I'd paid more attention to what Dad had told me about his research. Fiddling with my spoon, I tried to think of something intelligent to say. This could be the most exciting thing to happen all year. There'd be boat trips, hot PhD students and maybe even camping trips for fieldwork.

Dad arrived with Sean's coffee and a large whiskey.

'Liam, I was asking your daughter if she'd have the time to help us out,' Sean said as he poured the whiskey into his coffee and warmed his hands around the mug. 'I'll pay her a bit, of course,' he added, winking at me. 'Pocket money, like.'

'Jesus!' muttered Dad. I knew this was because of Sean pouring his whiskey into the coffee, one of my dad's snobbish pet hates, but Sean didn't notice the exclamation and stirred three packets of sugar into his drink as well. My dad's expression wasn't attractive.

'Oh, I don't know Sean, she's a lot of work to do.'

'Exams,' I gloomily stated. 'But I'll definitely have time to help you, too.'

Normally Dad would be dead set against anything that interfered with my schoolwork but I guessed that his love of the project would override that. So I sat up straight and gave him my loveliest smile. Apart from the thought of spending time with Sean, I really needed some money. I had to get a different phone and an iPad. My stupid dad didn't believe that a better phone on a different network might actually pick up a signal at the house.

'Please, Dad, it'd be so good for my CV,' I said.

He looked at Sean. 'What sort of thing would you want her to do?' he asked.

'Oh, a bit of this and that. The main thing is, she has a laptop. Clare can back up our own collations. Her brain's younger than ours.' He winked at me again. 'And we must be sure to be accurate.'

'Tell you what.' Dad said. 'You'll come up tonight, won't you? We can talk properly, then, about the whole thing.'

'Grand,' replied Sean, and added, 'I'm staying at the hostel though, with the others. But first, must go to the men's room.'

'Why's he staying at the hostel?' I whispered when Sean had gone.

'Ah, there is a group of field researchers from Norway staying there. Fish scientists. The project is being part-funded by the University of Trondheim and the Norwegian government. After all, our gannets and their gannets are all eating the same herring. Anyway, he'll be up later. I've to show him round the findings so far. Oh, and by the way, your mum's coming home on Friday.'

'Is she?' I looked at him wide-eyed. 'Why doesn't anyone ever tell me anything?'

Mum had been away in Dublin for six weeks, staying with my granny who had had a knee replacement. It had gone a bit wrong and she had been away far longer than we'd expected.

'I only found out last night myself. Your auntie Chrissie's come over from England to give her a break.' Dad shrugged and blew out a long sigh. 'Oh, and Nuala's coming, too.'

Nuala was mum's best friend and my godmother. I loved her. 'Brilliant, I haven't seen her for ages.'

'She's here till Tuesday, apparently.' Then he frowned. 'We'll have to tidy the place up, Clare.'

'You mean I'll have to tidy it up.' I groaned. But I didn't mean it. I couldn't wait to see Mum, and if Nuala was coming, and with Sean, too, it was going to be a fun weekend.

# 2: THE GLASS TOWER

Sean and I walked up the hill together, he pushing his bike and me trying to think of something interesting to say. I couldn't stop looking at him, and I couldn't work out what was so different about him. He'd changed from a spotty student with fluffy facial hair into a man. The beard made his bone structure seem somehow more defined. Seeing him again made me feel flustered and stupid.

He broke the silence: 'I've always meant to ask. Why is this place called The Old Brewery?'

'It used to be one,' I explained. 'The people who lived here before us made Biddle's Beer.'

As we rounded the corner I saw our house through Sean's eyes and felt quite proud of it. Sitting in the darkening sky on its birch-covered hummock, within the arms of the mountain, it looked like a fairy castle.

'Wow, has he finally finished the observatory?' he said. He took my arm as we trudged up the hill together.

'Yep,' I answered. 'Just before Christmas. Mum and I couldn't believe it.'

'It certainly is splendid,' said Sean. 'Worth the wait.'

We looked up at the circular tower. It sat separately, a stone's throw from the house. Dad had designed and built a glass observatory on top of the round brew house and it was famous amongst the local people, who thought Dad eccentric to build a glass tower in a place that was rocked by gale force winds for most of the year.

'It's beautiful, like a lighthouse,' Sean said.

'That was the idea. Dad's baby,' I said.

It had been a source of constant excitement to him during the planning and construction, with changes of plans and builders letting him down and so on. It had given us all a lot to talk about and I think it became all he talked about for a while. In fact, since the day he pronounced it finished, he'd hardly talked about anything at all.

At that moment our two dogs, Mac and Oscar, came charging round from the back of the house, barking at Sean but wagging their tails, filthy from chasing mice through the hedges and ditches.

'Oscar! Get down,' I shouted. He disobeyed me and jumped up again to lick my face. Mac stood calmly by with Sean stroking his head.

Dad must have heard the dogs because he opened the back door just as we arrived. I panicked. He didn't like me hanging around with his scientists. He said it was unprofessional for them to be disturbed by his household and anyway I should be studying, so that I could become a marine biologist like him.

'I'll take Sean up, Clare,' he stated.

I'd known this would happen, which was why I'd contrived the meeting by the lake.

'Will I bring some drinks up?' I asked hopefully.

'Get those dogs dried off first. Why did you let them out? They've already had their walk.'

I swore at him under my breath. Why did he always have to make me look stupid? Dad ushered his guest into the tower. I looked in through the doorway to watch Sean follow him up the spiral steps, and heard his gasp of amazement as he put his head up through the trapdoor opening. I then walked back towards the kitchen, kicking the gravel as I went.

With the dogs settled in their beds I put the kettle on for coffee, all the time thinking about whether Sean had really meant it about us working together. It would be so exciting to be doing something different, and I was sure Dad wouldn't mind if it helped the project.

My dad studied the effects of the moon and tides on marine life. The work was intensely boring to me. It seemed to focus on microscopic algae, krill and small aquatic worms. The most exciting thing he studied was herring. He could go on all day about the magical life cycle of the herring: how the old ones had amazing memories and led the younger ones to the best feeding grounds and how global warming was threatening their very survival. Their food was moving further north into cooler waters.

'What people don't understand, Clare,' he'd say as I stared at the wall, 'is that if the herring and all the other fish that depend on krill leave the area, it will devastate the birds, the seals and dolphins and the humans, too.'

I knew it was important but I'd heard him raging about it for so long now that it sailed over my head. However, with Sean's arrival, I decided to be fascinated by the life cycle of herring in a way I'd never been before.

I carried the coffee tray across the drive to the stone base of the tower, where I shouted from the bottom of the stairwell. Dad opened the trapdoor and took the tray from me. I had a horrible feeling he would then dismiss me so I barged my way past him before he could say anything.

Sean was still marvelling. I felt embarrassed for Dad at the state of the room. Every surface was covered in dust and dirty cups, and the wastepaper bin was hidden under a mountain of screwed up papers, banana skins and tea bags.

For all that, I did love being in the tower. The beeswax smell from the wooden floor evoked happy memories of Christmas. When Dad declared it finished, Mum strung it with fairy lights and we had a celebration with mulled wine and mince pies.

Sean stood in the middle looking up at the eight bevelled windows that curved overhead to form a celestial dome. Recessed lights illuminated a glittering drama, engraved into the roof glass, of fish being chased by diving sea birds and dolphins. I put the tray down onto my favourite window ledge where a mermaid sat gazing up at the dome.

When we first moved to the house, Dad told us that he'd always fancied living in a lighthouse and, as the brewery house was a round building, it was the perfect opportunity to make a glass dome. He had the brilliant idea of doing the dome in eight curved panels. It was a total obsession and he'd driven Mum crazy. She'd shouted at him that we were trying to settle in to a new place and all he could do was talk about his precious dome.

I think that was when things began to go wrong with our family. It seemed strange that as soon as the tower was finished mum had to go away. It was almost as though they didn't need each other any more.

Sean inspected Dad's telescope, lifting its funereal black cover to expose one of the many random pieces of optical equipment that Dad hoarded.

'Look,' Dad said. 'You can see breakers on Seal Island through this.' He polished the lens of the telescope with his shirtsleeve and moved aside for Sean.

I pointed out the Caher river estuary that fanned into the Atlantic and the harbour lights of Carran twinkling in the distance. Sean seemed delighted.

'You'll see it all better in the daylight,' Dad said.

'Show him with the light off, Dad.'

Dad switched off the lights and we all leaned our heads back to look up through the dome. The tiny amount of light from Venus's bright glow beside the thin moon was enough to make the dome gleam. Dad looked proudly at his creation as Sean marvelled some more

# 3: MORUS BASSANUS

Dad poured the coffee and we all sat facing the mermaid window.

'Apparently herring spawn after the last full moon in March,' I said in one breath. Sean swivelled round on his stool to look at me in surprise. Dad raised his eyebrows, too. I think this was where I scored a big point in my campaign to be allowed to work with Sean.

'I didn't know you cared! I'm a gannet man myself,' he said. 'I've been sent by CMRC this year, to study your local gannets.'

I knew that, and I knew that he certainly cared about herring. CMRC was the Coastal and Marine Research Centre at the University of Cork where all Dad's biologists came from.

'You know, your father's work is very important to us because when the herring and the other fish arrive, so do the birds.'

He began telling me all about the gannets.

'We reckon that the birds, who normally live further south on Little Skellig Island down in Kerry, have noticed on their feeding forays that there are a lot more fish up here. Whether it's due to overcrowding on Little Skellig or the abundance of fish here, it looks like they're trying to establish a new colony on the cliffs on Seal Island.' He smiled with child-like excitement. 'Over the last few summers, groups of young birds have been roosting and fishing up here. This year we predict a colony will be established.' He stood and paced from window to window, really excited now. 'This will be the first new gannet colony in Ireland since the thirties, imagine that, Clare. If your dad's herring arrive there's going to be enough fish for the gannets to feed themselves and their chicks for the whole summer.'

Despite Sean's ranting, which reminded me of Dad's, I found my interest in the big white bird growing. If the gannets nested locally, maybe Sean would stay, too.

'I'm going out to the island in the morning if you'd both like to come.'

'I can't,' Dad said. 'There's a man coming about the telephone lines, we keep being cut off.'

My heart sank until Sean looked questioningly at me.

'Oh, yeah, yes please. I'd love to, what time will I come?' I said it quickly so that Dad wouldn't have time to stop it. 'I've no actual lessons. I can catch up with revising in the evening. Dad, it's fieldwork!'

Eventually he agreed and we arranged that I'd be waiting on the quay at ten o'clock the following morning.

While Dad drove Sean back to Carran I curled up in bed with my dad's book: *The Atlantic Gannet, Morus bassanus*. It wasn't my usual bedtime reading but I needed to gen up to impress Sean.

# 4: SAOIRSE

I got on my bike and freewheeled down the steep back road to Carran. If you were a bird it was less than a mile away but the road meandered with the contours of the mountain and its foothills. I tried to avoid the potholes and when it became a muddy track I got off and walked the rest of it. The cobalt sea sparkled in the morning sun. There were no white caps on the waves so the water would be calm, though I certainly wasn't. After a long depressing winter with nothing but exams to think about, I couldn't get there fast enough. Out there, a new life might begin.

I arrived on the quay with twenty minutes to spare and, after propping my bike by the icehouse, sat on a mooring bollard to wait for Sean. I spotted *Saoirse*, a working lobster-fishing boat, moored at the end of the pier. Her skipper had an arrangement with the university and she was used for research support work as well as her usual job of setting and gathering in lobster and crab pots. As the lobster season hadn't started, the boat was usually available at this time of year.

Marine biologists, ornithologists, geologists, divers and occasional amateur fishermen would phone its skipper, Donal MacNamara, and he'd be only too glad to take their money. Donal and the other fishermen spent many a happy hour in The Atlantic, counting their money and laughing at the antics of the scientists. They'd give each other knowing smiles if some know-all from the university spent the trip seasick, with his head over the side of the boat.

A rusted and rattling silver Range Rover drove down to the end of the narrow pier. Donal and his son, Ronan got out and walked around a pile of discarded nets.

'Grand day for it,' said Donal, nodding over at me. I stopped staring down at the water and nodded back. 'Counting fish, are you?' he joked.

'Um, I'm going to the island to help with the project, with Sean O'Sullivan.'

Donal nodded and climbed down onto the deck, shouting at Ronan to bring his fish boxes from the boot.

'Hi, Clare,' Ronan murmured to me while opening the boot. He and his father would be going off to check their crab pots while we were on the island.

Ronan had been in my year at school, but he'd left at sixteen to work with his dad on the boat. Somehow he'd always felt a lot more grown up than my friends and me. He'd never really belonged to any group and we'd all thought him a bit odd.

Seeing him now with his dark hair and shy smile, I realised I'd never looked at him properly before. I saw the fine lines of his long legs in scuffed black jeans and the way his hair flicked in and out of the neck of his jumper as his strong arms grappled with the boxes.

I was about to offer him a hand when Sean freewheeled down the pier on one of the university hostel's bikes. It was very squeaky. In fact, I heard him before I saw him emerge from behind a stack of lobster pots. I stood up and straightened my jacket.

He propped the bike against the sea wall and walked over to *Saoirse*.

'Donal, how's it going?' The two men must have met in the pub the night before when Dad dropped Sean in town. They seemed very friendly.

'How's your head this morning?'

'It's been better, Donal,' replied Sean with a groan.

'He's a bad influence, Clare, and he's getting a good price for this con- sidering he's checking his pots at the same time.' I felt shy listening to the banter and noticed Ronan looking down at his boots, too.

'Come on, let's get this show on the road.' Donal said, to no one in particular.

Sean climbed down onto *Saoirse*'s wooden deck and held out a hand for me. Not wanting to appear pathetic, I ignored him and jumped down in one leap, slipping slightly but sliding to a halt without falling over.

The engine shuddered to life with a great cloud of diesel smoke and, as Ronan chucked the ropes down and came aboard, the little blue boat reversed and edged away from the harbour wall.

Sean stood chatting to Donal in the wheelhouse and Ronan went below decks to organise fishing gear. I wasn't used to being there without Dad so, though familiar with the boat, I felt a bit lost without him. Too shy to go forward to the bows where both men would be able to see me, I lingered at the back of the boat watching Carran get smaller as we chugged away.

I could hear them laughing about four Norwegian herring scientists who'd livened up the pub the night before. Apparently, they had followed numerous pints of lager with shots and ended up at Doughmore strand for a midnight swim. Everybody in the pub tried to stop them, as it's a dangerous beach and the water was freezing. The Norwegians wouldn't be stopped. Sean said he'd been relieved to hear them return to the hostel at four o'clock. They had been snoring away like bull seals as he stirred his breakfast porridge. And they had grunted in protest when Sean called them for the trip so he'd left them to sleep it off. I was disappointed when I heard that they wouldn't be on board with us.

Taking in great breaths of ozone-rich air, I smelled seaweed and diesel fumes, a mix that had always excited me. I loved joining my dad on the trips with the scientists and I'd been jealous because he'd been out to Seal Island with these Norwegians earlier that week when I was at school.

Dad said they had played a didgeridoo to some seals that had hauled out on a rock near the quay. The seals, fascinated by the music, had swum over to watch from a few metres away. I couldn't wait to meet the Norwegians. I hoped they might let me come to watch them call up the seals.

*Saoirse* followed the cliffs where shags and cormorants continuously spilled off the ledges. I loved watching the prehistoric birds skim low over the water, looking for food. Raucous croaks made me look up. A wheeling group of black birds tumbled through the sky above the cliffs. With their red legs and bills and constant shrieking and chattering, they were, to me, the most engaging members of the crow family. I guessed Sean would want to see them, too, so I went into the wheelhouse where the men were still laughing about the night before.

'Ah, hello Clare, how's it going?' Donal said.

'There's some choughs up above, I thought you'd ... '

Sean didn't speak but rushed past with his binoculars, ruffling my hair on the way out.

Donal winked at me. 'There's coffee in that bag, will you call Ronan and we'll all have some.'

I climbed down a steep ladder into the hold where Ronan, with his back to me, was untangling a bundle of damp ropes.

'Your dad says to come up for coffee.'

I had to shout above the hammering of the engine. He didn't hear me so I walked round in front of him and waved timidly. He jumped and then looked cross.

'Sorry,' I mumbled. 'It's just your dad said to tell you it's coffee time.'

'Jesus, Clare, I was miles away.' He dropped the ropes. I walked up the ladder ahead of him, acutely aware that as he climbed up behind me, his nose and my bum were inches apart. I rushed through the hatch, colliding with Sean.

'Well spotted, Clare. You always were good at noticing wildlife. I remember last year you always saw the dolphins before anybody else. And I haven't seen a chough since I was up in Donegal. You, my love, are going to be useful to me.' He hugged me and kissed the top of my head.

Forgetting all about Ronan, I leant against the starboard rail next to Sean. I could smell his damp wax jacket. The smell took me straight back to childhood. Mum had always worn wax coats.

I'd almost forgotten that my mum would be coming home the very next day. Still, there would be plenty of time later to get things ready. For now I had Sean's undivided attention. Together we peered at the cliffs until the choughs were out of sight. Then we went inside to join the others for coffee.

Leaving the shelter of the mainland, *Saoirse* made her way across the straits to Seal Island.

'North wind,' Sean commented.

'Unusual enough for the time of year,' replied Donal. 'Mind you, after all those westerly squalls last week, I, for one, am glad of a bit of dry weather.' He smiled at us all.

'Cold, though,' added Ronan. He was looking straight at me.

I loved the frosty clear light that came from the north. After months of gloomy dampness the cold was very welcome when it brought sunshine with it. Before I knew it, Donal had slowed the engine revs and the little quay on the island was alongside. Ronan jumped off and I threw him the mooring line, feeling oddly triumphant when he caught it and nodded at me.

'Welcome to Carrig na Ron,' he said, using the island's Irish name.

Sean passed a rucksack over to him and then stood back whilst I disembarked. With Ronan back on board and Sean standing next to me on the pier, *Saoirse* turned and chugged away out towards Donal's crab pots.

# 5: CARRIG NA RON

We stepped off the quay onto a shingle shore. The little beach gave way to small grassy dunes that would be covered in sea pinks during the summer months. The flowers weren't there now, just an old currach lying upside down on the sandy soil. The black-tarred canvas skin of the boat was old and tattered. It hadn't been to sea for a few years by the look of it.

A skinny brown dog appeared from behind a stack of lobster pots. She sniffed at a tangle of green fishing nets and then stood with her head lowered but ears pricked. I approached her, cautiously holding out my hand for her to sniff.

'Oh no, she's so thin,' I said. 'And look, she's had puppies.' Her teats were swollen.

'There shouldn't be dogs here.' Sean said. 'We'll have to move them.'

The dog ignored us but I couldn't help looking back at her as I followed Sean. She had intense yellow eyes, like a fox.

We walked up the only path on the island. It went more or less straight up from the beach to a group of ruined cottages. Some of them still had tatters of curtains blowing in the glassless windows. We looked in through the broken half door of the biggest one.

'It's so sad, isn't it?' I said, looking at a rusty bedstead that had been shoved into the fireplace. 'There must have been a range there once.'

Sean nodded to the collapsed gable end of the house. On top of the brambles that had woven up through the rubble, a robin warbled its fluted song.

'My dad said they all had to leave in the seventies. They used to make fiddles here and bring all their stuff back and forth by currach.' I looked up at him, expecting him to agree with me.

'Oh well, we have to move with the times, I suppose,' he replied.

'I wouldn't mind living here with the seals though, would you?' I asked, imagining us both living in the cottage.

'God no, it's much too far from the pub,' came his disappointing response.

I had a sudden flash of Ronan's face. The faraway look in his dreamy brown eyes and that shy smile. He would love to live here. Of that I was sure. I looked back at the sea, squinting into the sun. I was hoping to see the grey seals but they weren't there. I supposed that with last autumn's pups fending for themselves by now, the families would be out fishing at this time of day. Instead, I stood watching a crowd of peeping oystercatchers running up and down the shoreline.

'Come on, we've got things to do, birds to see.'

Sean took my arm in his and I forgot about the old cottage and snuggled into him away from the wind. We followed a steep stony trail up the island's only hill and stopped to catch our breath. From the top we could see the western edge of the hill that looked like it had been blasted away by a bomb.

'Look how the sea erodes everything,' he said. 'You can see where a great chunk must have collapsed into the sea.'

There was nothing left of it now. Stone stacks and cliffs filled the space where the side of the island had been claimed by the Atlantic.

Great swirls of green water crashed against the rocks, throwing spray fifty feet into the air.

'I reckon that's where Team Gannet predict the birds will nest.'

'Team Gannet?' I asked.

'Yeah, me and the guys who predicted the gannets' behaviour; it's what we call ourselves.'

Sean pointed at a huge flattened slab that jutted up from a rocky outcrop on their left side. Holding his binoculars up to his eyes he exclaimed: 'Yes!' in a loud voice.

He passed me the glasses and began walking down towards the cliffs to get a better look.

'Careful, it'll be slippery,' I shouted and then looked through the binoculars. There were sombre-looking shags, pretty kittiwakes and a few guillemots huddling against the wind.

'Can you see them?' Sean shouted back up at me.

'No, I don't think so,' I said, straining my eyes.

'Over there! They're juveniles.'

Of course, I remembered from the book that the young gannets don't gain their pure white plumage until their third or fourth year. These would be early explorers recently arrived back from their migration to Africa. Standing on the outcrop, in the windiest part of the cliffs, stood six dark mottled birds. They were as big as geese and almost invisible next to the black rock.

'I can see them,' I shouted with excitement, glad to be sharing this with Sean. And I couldn't wait to tell Dad. Perhaps I, too, was now a part of Team Gannet.

We arrived back on the shingle just as *Saoirse* reversed up to the quay. Ronan jumped off to take the mooring lines.

'There are sandwiches if you want some,' he said in a low voice.

Back on board I nearly tripped over a box of crabs. They clacked about uselessly, their claws tied with elastic bands.

Sean spent a while out on deck asking Donal questions and picking up the crabs to inspect their undersides. I couldn't bear to look at their waving legs, so I followed Ronan into the wheelhouse for lunch. He passed me a foil packet of soggy cheese and tomato sandwiches, which we sat eating while he took the wheel. He didn't say a word.

Back in Carran Dad was waiting on the pier. Donal tucked *Saoirse* in between two small trawlers and threw a rope up to him. The tide was fully out so the boat's roof was level with Dad's boots.

I scuttled up a ladder to the roof and jumped across to the harbour wall, where we stood watching Ronan and Donal dragging the crab box to the edge of the boat.

'Can I give you a hand, Donal?' Dad asked.

'No Liam, no need, we'll be grand,' Sean shouted up. 'You go ahead to the pub but it's my round, I'll help Donal here first.'

I put my bike into the boot of Dad's wonderfully warm car and we drove up to the town.

'Go and grab that table,' Dad pointed over to the window. I waited for him with my hands stretched out to warm in front of the turf fire.

'What time's Mum coming tomorrow?' I asked when he joined me.

'She said it'd be mid-morning but you know her,' he replied. 'We'll have the place ready for eleven or so.' His eyes brightened at the thought. 'We'll go and get some shopping in now for her, anyway, shall we?'

I nodded and looked at the fire. I did feel sorry for my dad. He loved it when my mum was home but he always seemed lonely even when she was there. My parents never seemed to laugh any more.

# 6: LIGHTING THE FIRES

I woke early the next morning. I'd been dreaming about Ronan.

*We're swimming together and have dived down to look at the seabed where the crabs live. He's holding my hand and that's given me the power to breathe underwater.*

Lying there with my eyes half open, I imagined him being one of the seal people that locals said came from the islands. I'd a vague memory that his mother may have been from the island. She'd died before we arrived in the area but I'd no idea why. I wondered if Dad knew.

I woke up properly, remembered Mum and swore when I saw the clock. I'd overslept. I jumped out of bed to open the curtains. Condensation ran down the cold windowpanes. A heavy hoar frost had coated the bare trees. It reminded me of the scenes Mum and I used to make on our homemade Christmas cards, dripping with glue and too much glitter. The kitchen garden had raspberry cane icicles and frozen fountains of leeks and cabbages. I'd never seen such a heavy frost.

Down in the kitchen I found Dad lighting the range. 'We'll get the fires going for your mum,' he said, without looking up.

Watching him bent over the task with his long legs creased into an awkward shape I felt sorry for him. 'Shall I finish that one?' I asked.

'Yes, please do,' he said, straightening up with a series of creaks and groans. 'Can you do that one and the one in the living room? I'll go and get more wood in. Oh, and perhaps we should get the bedroom fire going as well in case your mum wants a lie down.'

I suddenly regretted my offer of help. Three fires to light and no doubt he'd expect me to tidy the house, as well.

'Can we have breakfast first?' I asked.

'We'll do this first, you know how long it takes to warm the place.' He flicked an ingratiating smile at me on his way out to the wood-barn.

He returned, minutes later, dragging a box of logs. Behind him, a small damp whirlwind of dogs exploded into the kitchen. Oscar raced over and jumped up to greet me. I shouted at him to get down, then relented and let him carry on his feverish licking and leaping.

'Let's dry this lot off,' Dad said, which meant, 'you towel the mud off them'.

Eventually I sat at the table eating toast in the warm, tidy house. Late morning sun sent dusty rays through the kitchen where the dogs stretched and sighed in front of the range. My dad had gone back out to split more logs.

Every morning he took the dogs and went up our mountain to get wood. Sometimes I went with him but I hadn't been for ages. In among the plantation pines there were remnants of old woodland. A yew hedge, on the north edge of the garden, had been allowed to grow into a maze of strangely shaped trunks and overhanging branches that could have been a rath: a fairy fort. My mum said it maybe was a rath and that we should leave offerings to the fairies for good luck. She was only joking but I liked to think it was true.

I walked to the wood-barn through the stand of winter birches that surrounded the house. With their white velvet trunks and slender leafless arms it felt like part of a fairy fort, too. The door to the barn was open and I sat on a log, breathing in pine resin perfume, watching Dad and daydreaming. He looked pleased with himself, working his axe amidst a growing heap of split logs.

We were so engrossed that we didn't hear her car until it braked in the gravel. Throwing down his axe he turned towards the door just as I ran over from the stump I'd been sitting on. We stood together, a small welcoming committee, and watched the shiny black door of the car as it opened. Mum was home.

# 7: ORLA'S RETURN

Dad pulled her towards him. She pecked his cheek and let him fold her into his arms. I could smell her as he crushed her like a petal, releasing her fragrance. Cigarette smoke mixed with perfume.

She looked thinner, fragile and bony. Her dark brown hair was pulled into a chignon with loose wisps coiled around her ears. Her hazel eyes, made up to look even bigger than they were, closed for a few moments. She was nervous and fidgety in his arms, like a cat that doesn't want to be picked up.

She opened her eyes and looking over his shoulder at me, suddenly ducked out of his embrace.

'Hey, love,' she said. Her hug was so intense that I thought she'd snap one of my ribs. Then she pushed me back to arm's length and looked me up and down.

'You look different, sweetheart, are you ok?'

I looked down at my mother's shoes. Shiny court shoes that looked incongruous on the gravel. What could I say? I never felt ok. I'd been really missing her, worrying about Dad and wondering why she didn't come home. My auntie was supposed to have come home from England to help out as well but she hadn't been able to get away until this weekend. It had been a long time, and although Mum kept saying I should come to stay with her, somehow that never happened.

I couldn't help thinking that she stayed in Dublin more than she had to. Surely someone else could have granny-sat for her. I also wondered why Dad didn't suggest that we both went to see her. They just didn't seem to like each other very much any more. Anyway, I just wished she wouldn't ask me how I was.

'I'm fine,' I lied. Mum hugged me again.

'I'll bring in your things, love.' Dad, having already opened the boot, was standing looking into it, wondering where to start. Mum had been shopping. Seriously shopping.

Together we began emptying the car. Mum always brought presents when she came home. And, as usual, there was a mountain of supplies from the Dublin shops. I helped bring everything to the kitchen, peering into the boxes to see what was there.

The dogs met her as she opened the door to the warm kitchen. Oscar and Mac were bouncing up and down like pogo sticks. When, for the third time, Mum's pale skirt was marked with a dirty paw, she shouted 'Enough!' with such authority that both dogs ran under the table and sat there panting, looking sideways at the wall.

'Can you put these away, love, while I go and change?' she asked.

'Then we'll have some lunch,' added Dad.

'Don't open those,' said Mum pointing to a pink bag with roses on it and a huge white SALE bag from a man's clothes shop. She followed Dad out through the kitchen door.

While they disappeared, I had time to inspect every little thing that she'd bought.

Our two fat tabby cats materialised as if by magic. They had one thing on their radars: the food in those boxes. Smoked fish was the cause of the twitching noses. I picked up the damp package, enjoying its cool waxy weight. I had a good sniff before putting it safely away in the fridge. The salty smell reminded me of New Year. We'd had brown bread and local salmon and a bottle of champagne. My dad would have said: 'Coals and Newcastle springs to mind,' but I knew the package was Mum's symbol of happy days.

With the fish safely stowed there should have been no further reason for interest from the two cats but they weaved a dance around the bags and boxes and me. Eventually, with a rather violent movement, I shoved them off the table and poured biscuits into a bowl to distract them. That alerted the dogs and I had to give them some, too. This was against the rules but who cared? By the time my parents returned the evidence would have been eaten.

In the box where the fish had been, I found avocados, peppers, plum tomatoes, basil, pomegranates and big sunny lemons. Underneath these unseasonal Mediterranean treasures was a jumble of garlic and fat red onions, tubs of olives and anchovies and other salty, juicy things.

It was hard to get these in Carran and Mum loved cooking. When I was little we had to move around a lot to keep up with Dad's work. Mostly it was Scotland or Ireland, but there were three years when we island hopped around the Mediterranean because of migrating sardines. Wherever we lived in the sardine years, Mum found the best markets and shops. I loved watching her try out new recipes with a glass of wine in one hand and a wooden spoon in the other, her face glowing in the alchemy of experimentation and steam. Whenever she went to Galway or Dublin she came home with a car full of exciting ingredients for cooking.

I threw the cardboard box into the firewood alcove and ripped open the next one. Everything would be put away at the end, but I loved seeing it all spread out on the table, like a picture from a holiday brochure.

'Mmmmm, this is good,' I told the dogs. Oil splashed over my fingers as I slurped a huge green olive, smacking my lips and licking my fingers, with four pairs of eyes looking on with great interest.

I pushed the empty box to one side and turned my attention to a paper bag of bread and cheeses. I couldn't resist tearing the end of one of the plump loaves, chewing it with a groan of pleasure that set the dogs off wagging and panting in anticipation. Licking flour from my lips, I put it and the cheeses into the large old pantry that had once been the happy home of Mrs. Biddle's jams and pickles.

Three cases of French wine filled the remainder of the boxes. Dad was always telling Mum that it was possible to buy food in Carran but she couldn't help herself. It did occur to me that this was a particularly good haul. Such extravagance could only mean one thing. Mum had plans for a party.

Putting aside the presents, I cleared a space on the sideboard under the window and began breaking eggs into a bowl. Staring out at the dripping vegetables in the now sunny and thawing kitchen garden, I considered the perfect omelette I'd make. Mum and Dad would be impressed and that was a good feeling. I smiled at Oscar who was wagging his tail beside me and began whisking the eggs into froth.

Next, I prepared the espresso machine Mum had brought for Dad two Christmases ago. He was more of a tea man so it only came out of its cupboard when she was at home. I smiled, imagining Mum's face when she realised how accomplished her daughter had become in the kitchen since she'd been away.

They were taking ages. The coffee grew cold as I sat waiting at the table, looking at the eggs slowly separating in their bowl.

When they returned, they looked like different people. Dad wore a jacket instead of his usual jumper and Mum had discarded her grey city suit and neat heels. Instead she had on a bright red skirt and sheepskin boots. Her dark hair, loosened from its clip, rippled down her back and she had her silver hoop earrings on. Dad often said she was a gypsy at heart and she certainly looked the part now. But her eyes and nose were red and dried tears had streaked her face.

Dad stared at the range.

'I'll go and get more wood,' he muttered and whistled for the dogs to follow.

'Let's get the lunch done,' said Mum briskly. 'Christ, where is everything? Every time I turn my back it's all changed.' She searched the dresser for cutlery to lay the table.

'I know,' I said, glad of a change of atmosphere. 'It's Dad, he's always moving things around.'

'Housekeeping's never been his strength, you know. When I first met him, his bathroom was a photographic darkroom, I'd have to wee in a bowl in the kitchen because he wouldn't let me in.' She smiled and gazed out of the window, then put her hand on my arm. 'I've a present for you.'

She passed me the pink-roses bag. It was held together with wide purple ribbon. I squeezed the bag, knowing it was clothes. My mother always thought I looked gorgeous in the sort of clothes that she herself liked wearing. Her tastes were ethnic and colourful or else tailored and formal. She was always lecturing me about this.

'Show off your assets, you've got great legs and fabulous boobs.'

I absolutely did not want anyone seeing my legs nor noticing the shape of my breasts. I felt just about comfortable in jeans and t-shirts and big jumpers. I'd told Mum this again and again.

'But you live in your wetsuit all summer and that certainly shows off your assets.'

That may have been true but under water I was hidden and felt more at home anyway. Sure enough, Mum had done it again. It was a midnight blue, knee length, velvet dress. If I'd been seven I'd have been ecstatic. I could only feel hurt that she'd got it so wrong.

'Mmmm, thanks, it's lovely.' I looked down at it not wanting to catch her eye.

'I wasn't sure it was what you'd like but that colour has always looked perfect on you,' she said with a big smile. 'You can wear it tomorrow night. I've friends coming. We're having a party.'

Dad came in, dragging his log box. The dogs followed, joyfully wagging their tails and sticking their noses into Mum's crotch. She brushed them aside and began picking mugs down from the dresser. Apart from the intense stares of the cats, nobody looked at anybody.

The re-filled coffee machine began to hiss. We all stood watching it and then Mum poured herself a cup.

'Going out for a ciggie.' Mum smiled but wouldn't look at anyone. To my horror a tear was running down her cheek. We watched her walk across the garden and place her mug on top of the sundial. Standing with her head bowed, she cupped her hands to light her cigarette, then leaned back and slowly exhaled. A stream of blue smoke sat in the air. The sun had warmed the ground but coldness in the air made her breath come out in puffs that mingled with the steam from her coffee.

When she turned back towards the window, I busied myself with tidying the table and putting away the food.

'What've we got here then?' my father asked with a cheerful tone. Good old Dad, always trying to brighten things up.

On the draining board, the bowl of whisked eggs sat congealing. 'It's for an omelette, shall I start it?' I said, with a worried glance out of the window at Mum's stooped shoulders.

'I don't see why not.' Dad frowned and looked into the garden again.

Mum was walking around looking at the fruit bushes and roses. I knew she'd be cross that Dad still hadn't pruned them. She was always trying to get me and Dad involved in the garden and had left detailed instructions about the pruning, which neither of us had remembered.

She came back in to find me laying the table and Dad fiddling with the radio. She looked better, no trace of tears, her face pale again but for a faint blush on her cheeks from the cold air.

'I bought you something.' She handed him the big white bag.

Unlike me, he never worried about her presents. She had perfect taste as far as he was concerned. It was a Donegal tweed jacket. He peeled back the tissue paper and ran his fingers over the soft fabric and leather buttons. It was tobacco brown with a green fleck, which Mum said she knew would bring out the green in his eyes.

'Try it on, Dad, it's lovely,' I said brightly, trying to cheer the sombre mood.

'Later, love,' he said as he kissed Mum on the cheek. 'Thank you, it's very nice,' he added.

I served them my rubbery omelette and sat down to eat. The dogs stayed in their baskets instead of waiting under the table for scraps.

# 8: CAIT AND THE HORSES

After lunch I left my parents in the kitchen and went up to my bedroom. I'd been so excited about Mum coming home that I'd forgotten how tense it could be. Throwing the pink bag onto the bed I changed into old jeans and ran back down to the kitchen. Mum sat at the table with her hand on top of Dad's. He was frowning at the top of her bowed head.

'I'm just going down the road. Can I bring Cait if we're having a party?'

'Yes, of course you can, love. Tell Maggie Nuala's coming, will you,' replied Mum with a weak smile. Plainly, she'd been crying again.

I got my bike from the turf shed and rode down the long slope to the lakeside. Evening was coming around the frozen lake. The pines on the north side were in deep shadow while the hawthorn on the south side glowed red in low sun. I couldn't wait to see Cait.

Cait was my nearest neighbour and my best friend. She lived with her mum, Maggie, in a farm down the hill from us. We usually went to school together, either by bike or with a lift from my dad or her mum. Her birthday was in August, exactly a week before mine, and we were the youngest two in our class.

When I reached Cait's, Maggie was in the yard trying to round up her hens, dressed in a bright hand knitted jumper, an embroidered Indian print skirt and a pair of very muddy black wellingtons. Her hair looked as though it hadn't been brushed but was tied up with a red scarf to keep it from flopping into her eyes. She was all flustered and flapping, looking a bit like a hen herself.

'Hi Clare, how are you, love?' She said.

'Hello, yeah, ok. Mum's home.'

'Oh, is she? That's great news, is her mother out of hospital at last?'

I said I didn't know. I hadn't thought to ask.

'Listen, there's supposed to be more frost later so I'm getting this crowd in early, will you give me a hand?' She told me where to stand to stop the chickens from running away and despite interference from Spats, her white footed terrier, the feathery bundles were soon rustling about on the straw in their wooden house.

'Where's Cait?' I asked.

'She's up haying the horses. Come in, we'll get some tea ready. She'll be on her way back by now.'

I thought about going to meet Cait but the cosy farmhouse kitchen was more tempting.

Cait and her brother had been young children when their dad died in a farming accident. Cait never talked about it so I wasn't really sure what actually happened. All I knew was that Maggie had brought them up on her own. As well as chickens and horses, she kept a few sheep. She was always juggling her money and sometimes did cleaning jobs to make ends meet.

'Come in, Clare,' she said. 'You haven't been down for ages and the house is so quiet with Tom away at college. I do so miss the sound of you young people laughing and listening to your music.' Maggie cleared clutter from the table and laid out mugs and plates.

'Mum's home for the weekend,' I repeated. 'She said to say she's having a party tomorrow so to come up.' I stroked Spats, who was standing on my knees.

'Just what the doctor ordered, I've been missing your mum and dad's parties, will there be music?'

'Well, I know Mum's got Nuala and other friends from Dublin and Dad's bound to ask the Healeys, so there should be music.'

A young woman in bright pink wellingtons and a very muddy riding coat burst through the door.

'Clare! Yay!' Cait pulled her bobble hat off and a shock of short blond hair stuck out in all directions. 'Hang on, just need to take my boots off.' She dropped her coat on the floor inside the door.

'God, Mum, it's freezing up there, the water trough's frozen solid. Goblin tried to follow me home, I wish we could have some stables for them.'

'Please don't start that again, we can't afford it and horses have been living outside for millions of years.'

'But it would be so lovely to see their heads over the stable doors in the morning,' Cait implored.

'Cait, you know you're wasting your breath. When you've your own place you can build a palace for them but for now...'

I sat back, relishing the warm messy kitchen and the family squabble. Mum used to argue with me, but lately we just had polite phone calls to each other. Dad liked telling me off but never argued like that. He was usually too distracted with his own thoughts. Even Mum and Dad never argued any more. They just had horrible silences. It was as though we were all too scared to say anything out of turn, in case one of us said something we might regret. Like, is Mum really away because of Granny? Or is someone not telling me something? Cait and her mum were always shouting at each other but they were always laughing and joking, too.

'Is Tom coming home soon?' Cait's brother had gone away to agricultural college.

'He's got to be back for lambing, which should start in a week or so.' Maggie glanced at the Jack Russell Terriers calendar Tom had given her for Christmas.

'I miss him,' I said.

'I know, love, we all do.' Maggie sighed.

'I don't miss his horrible music,' added Cait.

'Well, I think it's just too quiet around here without him.' Maggie poured water from the kettle into her teapot.

Maggie and Cait were small and fair but Tom was different. From a photo of his father on the wall, standing with a baby in one hand and an upside down boy dangling from the other, you could see he'd been a tall, broad man. It felt wrong that someone so big and strong could be dead. Tom was six foot two, dark and slightly overweight, fond of his food and his beer and good at giving bear hugs.

Maggie put the teapot on the table. I loved that teapot. How many times had I warmed my hands on its brown belly?

'We've twenty ewes to lamb, tell your dad I'll phone when it starts,' she said, pouring the tea.

'He'll be really pleased to help,' I said. 'Oh, but he's got the gannet thing this spring as well.' I told them all about Sean and Team Gannet, and our visit to the island. I was waiting for some time alone with Cait to tell her about Ronan, too. We drank our tea and ate Maggie's crumbly apple cake that was still warm from the oven.

'S'pose I should get back.' I had a good stretch and yawned.

'You look like your mother, Clare. Sometimes you could be sisters.' Maggie smiled at me and got up from the table.

'I'll walk up with you to the lake.' Cait offered.

'Can you girls take a brick to the horse trough and break the ice on it?' Maggie cleared a space on the cluttered table and began peeling vegetables.

We put on our coats and boots and I borrowed some gloves for the icy weather outside.

On the walk I told Cait all about Ronan. She remembered him from school but took a bit of persuading that he'd turned into a *sex god*. Then I found myself asking her what she knew about him. I didn't grow up in Connemara like she did so I always had to rely on her for local knowledge.

'He seems really shy.' I said.

'Or maybe he's just unfriendly. All I know is that he's an only child and his mum died when he was about six, I think. So it's just him and his dad.'

'Has he got a girlfriend?' I tried to sound offhand.

'God no, well, he's a bit weird, isn't he?' Cait laughed as she spoke.

'Yeah, I suppose. Maybe because he doesn't have a mum.'

We walked over to the trough, comparing observations on every boy we knew and laughing so much that I slipped on the ice and landed on my bottom in the half frozen mud.

# 9: THE VISITORS

I left Cait and walked my bike back up the steep hill to the house. Lights from the tower illuminated a car parked on the frosty gravel. Dad must have added turf to the fire: I could smell its comforting peaty musk. I supposed the car must belong to Mum's friends and crept in the back way to change out of my jeans.

I decided on my black skirt and top and black tights, brushed my hair and put make-up on. Examining myself in the mirror I sprayed the perfume Mum had given me for Christmas. I thought I looked just about presentable but was nervous at the thought of visitors.

Everybody turned when I entered the kitchen. Oscar and Mac jumped joyfully from their beds, which was a relief as it distracted me from the warm tableau of merrymaking around me. Mum had her head thrown back, laughing with gusto at Dad and Sean who were in mid anecdote about the Norwegian scientists. Nuala was there with two people I'd never seen before. The 'no smoking in the house' rule must have been lifted because I could hardly breathe for the haze of tobacco smoke. The table was a jumble of glasses and half empty wine bottles.

'Darling, it's great to see you.' Nuala, in acres of moss green linen and ropes of amber beads, stood up. I let her engulf me in familiar, sandalwood-scented arms.

'Look at you, even more grown up.'

I hadn't seen her since the summer before when Mum and I visited her huge Georgian house in Dublin. Had I really changed so much since then?

'So, Clare, your dad says you're planning to be a famous scientist just like him.' She winked at Dad.

Aware of Sean watching with interest, I tried to think of something impressive to say.

'Yes, I'm quite interested in marine biology but I'm not really sure.' That didn't sound at all impressive. I looked at Sean who was nodding at me, as though willing me to go on.

'She's helping me on the gannet project, for starters,' he said kindly.

'Although we're not quite sure what she'll do.' Dad walked over and put a possessive arm around me.

'We'll have a chat, darlin', when you've the time.' Nuala blew me a kiss.

'Glass of wine, love? I think you're old enough now.' Mum smiled as she waved the bottle at me.

I didn't really like red wine and was offended by Mum's assumption that I was only just old enough to drink, but grateful that at least she'd included me with the adults. As I went to the cupboard to get a glass, Mum stood to introduce me.

'Clare, this is Gerry and Jeanette. They're journalists. You might like to chat to them about your career plans.'

I didn't know what to say, so just stood there nodding and smiling.

'Your hands are freezing.' Jeanette, a petite woman with a chestnut bob and a smart black trouser suit, grasped both of my hands in hers.

'I've been down helping my friend with her horses.' I explained about the frozen water trough.

'Come and sit by the range, won't you?' said Gerry, moving his chair back from the table. Suddenly I was part of the cosy group around the table. Gerry, bearded and laughing, was pressed right next to me, and Sean squeezed onto the end of the table at my other side. I tried not to grimace at the vinegary taste of the wine.

'You look a bit pale, love.' Nuala put her glasses on and scrutinised me.

'Oh, I'm fine, you know. Working hard and stuff.' I glanced away to the window to hide my face. Nuala always seemed to know what I was thinking and I couldn't face a heart-to-heart no matter how well meaning it was. Mainly because, though I didn't know why, I would be bound to cry.

'Sean's been telling us all about your gannet project,' said Gerry. 'I told him we'd love to do an article about it. Perhaps you could help us. You know, be our Seal Island Correspondent. We could find a slot for it somewhere in the schedule.'

I laughed. Mum seemed to know a lot of people in telly and journalism. It wasn't the first time her friends had invited me to help with a story. Sometimes it earned me some money. Last summer Cait and I had helped write a Sunday article with Maggie about the lonely struggles of a woman sheep farmer. We made a hundred Euros each and all went to Galway shopping for the day.

'Let's hope we've something worth writing about.' Sean interrupted.

'Whatever happens we'll have a story about where the herring are spawning,' said Dad.

'Not quite as cuddly as gannets,' said Jeanette.

'Yes, but global warming's a hot subject, you know?' Dad was not going to give in. He was fed up with people not taking his research seriously.

'Liam, will you, for God's sake, stop being the prophet of doom. Let's get some food organised, shall we?' Mum glared at him briefly, stubbed out her cigarette, pushed her chair back, yawned and stretched her arms up to the ceiling.

'We'll go up to the tower, folks.' Dad drained his glass and led Gerry and Jeanette, who hadn't seen the tower, with Sean out through the hallway towards the spiral stairway.

'Don't let that fire go out, Clare,' he shouted back over his shoulder.

Mum opened a window to clear the fug while Nuala tidied the table.

'I've made a lasagne for everybody.' Mum opened the fridge door and began pulling out all the stuff I'd stowed away earlier. 'But we need to sort out a salad.'

'Lovely,' said Nuala. 'Tell me what to do.'

'First, we need more wine.' Mum closed the window again and gave me a hug. 'I'm so happy to be here with my two favourite people,' she said as she squeezed me and then turned to Nuala.

'It's great to be here with you, Orla.' Nuala returned Mum's hug. 'And your lovely daughter. Look at her. She's gorgeous. You must come up to Dublin to stay with me soon, Clare.'

We sat round the table chopping vegetables, nibbling olives, and gossiping about everybody we knew.

'Put the plates to warm, Clare, and get some of that bread out,' Mum said.

I obediently opened the pantry door. 'Who's coming for the party, Mum?'

She didn't answer and was staring into mid-air with a wooden spoon in her hand, seeming very distracted. She sighed and turned her head back to the bubbling pot just as the men and Jeanette returned. Before long we all sat round our table eating. As they laughed at each other's anecdotes I felt a bit left out with nothing to tell.

'I'd better go and study, I've an essay to do before Monday.' Everyone protested but I knew they wouldn't miss me for long. Sean didn't even look up from his conversation.

When I left the room Dad was deep in conversation with Gerry about herring stocks. Nuala was trying not to laugh, watching Sean impersonating Dad. It was quite funny but I felt it unfair, really. Adults were so like children when they'd had a drink. Mum and Jeanette were standing in front of the open kitchen window smoking and bitching about people they knew in Dublin. Even the dogs didn't notice me leave.

# 10: SNOW DAY

I didn't sleep very well that night and kept waking with the duvet twisted around me. I had loads of dreams but one in particular stood out.

*Sean and Nuala are laughing at me. Then Nuala's amber beads are seaweed and I'm floating in the bay on Seal Island. A dark shape in the water becomes Ronan swimming past. With his dark hair plastered to his head he looks like a sea creature. As he turns towards me he's a seal with a muzzle full of whiskers and sloe black eyes. I swim towards him and we dive deeper and deeper into a strong current that frightens me and sweeps me up out of sleep.*

When I woke I felt a great sense of yearning and found myself crying but didn't know why. Mum would have said it was my hormones but it felt like more than that.

I must have slept again because the dogs woke me up barking in the kitchen garden underneath my window. I could hear their claws clacking on the path as they tore round to the front of the house. Then there were crunching steps in the gravel and Mum shouted at someone, probably the dogs, and a door slammed. I turned over in bed and lay looking at my curtains. They had an embossed leaf pattern but I could see hundreds of tiny seals swimming through them. Milky light and the sound of people clattering up and down the stairs eventually pulled me out of bed.

Throwing back the curtains I couldn't believe my eyes. It was snowing. Nothing had settled but the flakes looked feathery and dry. The sky was dark with heavy clouds that I prayed were full of snow, not rain. I hadn't seen snow since we lived in Scotland and I couldn't wait to find Cait to go sledging. Not that we had a sledge but Dad would make something for us. At least I'd a good reason to wear layers of jumpers and my scruffiest, most comfortable trousers. Suddenly I was starving and ready for a big breakfast.

Apple-wood smoke and the smell of freshly brewed coffee infused the warm breakfast hubbub in the kitchen. Dad was feeding the range with the wood he'd split the day before. It came from a bough that had dropped off our apple tree in the kitchen garden. It crackled as it burned, and filled the room with a wonderful spicy mulled-wine smell.

Mum stood by the sink, refilling the cafetiere. Nuala, Gerry and Jeanette were quietly eating scrambled eggs. Mum turned to talk to me.

'Clare, love, breakfast?' She pushed the coffee plunger down and poured coffee for everybody except Dad. She then gestured to me with the pot.

'Coffee? Toast? Eggs? What would you like?'

Mum didn't usually ask me what I wanted for breakfast. I said I'd get some cereal. Dad moved away from his position in front of the range to let me pass. He kept running his hands through his hair so that it stood out in all directions.

'Isn't this great?' The backdoor flew open and Sean appeared with a snowball that he pretended to put down Mum's cardigan.

She squirmed and ran outside where she stood with her arms out, hands upturned and tongue hanging out to catch the falling snow. Dad followed her out and offered her one of her own cigarettes. She accepted it and they walked off around the garden. I made myself some tea.

'I've to take Sean down to Carran. Is there anything you folk need?' Dad said when they returned, looking at Gerry and Nuala.

'Can I come? Please,' I said. Maybe, by some miracle, Ronan would be there.

'I wouldn't mind a look around,' added Nuala.

Thank goodness Jeanette insisted on doing the washing up. I ran upstairs to put on some make-up. Then I tore off my scruffy jeans and swapped the sports bra I'd put on for sledging for my push-up one. On the way out I saw my side view in the mirror and groaned. Why did I have to be so dumpy? Dad was tall and Mum was so elegant. What had happened to me?

Outside my window, the kitchen garden had turned into a Christmas card complete with a robin on the iced roof of the bird table and two dogs sneezing as they nose-ploughed the snow. Mum and Dad stood watching them. I saw him try to put his arm onto her shoulder. She shrugged him off and walked away.

# 11: SNOWBALL

Snow was beginning to coat the trees and lie in the fields. Driving down by the main road, I could see Maggie's sheep with a white dusting on their fleeces and noticed that someone had put rugs onto Goblin and Damson. The horses had their heads down in a pile of hay with their bottoms to the wind.

'Oh, Dad,' I'd forgotten to tell him. 'Maggie says it's lambing from next week, probably, and can you help? I told her you were busy with the gannet project, though.'

'Lambing time again already. We'll call in to see if they need anything from the town.' Dad reversed into the farm gateway.

The hens were still cooped up from the night before and nobody answered the door, but there was smoke coming out of the farmhouse chimney and lights on in the kitchen.

Shrill yipping alerted us to a little snowstorm that skidded around the corner of the barn. Spats rushed up and nipped Sean on the calf.

'Jaysus!' He shouted, kicking the yapping dog away. Spats, landing in a heap and righting himself in a second, bounced up into my face with his tongue darting out for a quick lick. I shouted at him and carefully felt my newly made-up face.

'Hang on, folks,' said Dad. 'Clare, go see if they're in the lambing shed.' Dad held the others back.

I looked quietly around the half open barn door and couldn't help letting out a loud 'Aaaaah'. Maggie had her hand inside the back end of a ewe and Cait squatted in the straw next to her, rubbing a pair of lambs to keep them warm.

'Come over.' Cait beckoned to me. 'She's having triplets, the ram must have got to her early, Mum doesn't know how.' With a loud bleat the ewe strained and Maggie's hand emerged with two hind legs in her grip. Then, with a rush of waters and blood, something slithered out and lay still on the straw. The shiny dark lump looked all rotten and dead. Then, as Maggie rubbed it, the wet chest started heaving and a little mouth opened. It was a black lamb half the size of its siblings, but definitely alive.

'Well, that's a rare sight.' Maggie's knees cracked as she stood up and retied her scarf, which had fallen into the straw. 'Three lambs and a black one, too,' she said. 'I can't think who got to her, must've been one of McGuan's rams. I swear I'll kill him one day.'

Maggie had a special breed of sheep called Galways. They were pure white with a long coat for spinning wool. But McGuan's were all black-faced mountain sheep and his rams were always escaping.

'He never fences his land properly, and in any case they'd scale a wall to reach one of Maggie's ewes,' said Dad, who had crept in behind me.

'And my pedigree ram doesn't get a look in with his crowd running wild. This ewe's conceived at least a week earlier than the others.' Maggie bent down to scoop up the black lamb. 'She won't cope with three, we'll have to hand rear this one.'

Cait and I were delighted. It was Cait's job to hand rear the orphan lambs and she always asked me to help her. 'Let's go and make him a bed,' she said. We took the quivering bundle from Maggie and left her trying to get the white lambs suckling from her exhausted ewe. Dad, walking ahead of us, had taken Sean and Nuala into the kitchen. He opened up the range to encourage a good blaze for boiling the kettle. I closed the door quietly behind us all.

'Ah God, look at that.' Nuala stood and peered down at the damp little face. The lamb mewed as she poked her little finger in between its lips. Following Cait's instructions, I found a cardboard box and some old towels. There was also a scruffy sheepskin that Maggie kept for the orphans.

'Here, you take him.'

Although he was wet I wrapped him in a towel and pushed him inside my coat to keep warm while Cait heated up some frozen sheep's milk and poured it into a bottle. She handed it to me and everybody crowded round to watch his little mouth close around the teat and start to suck.

'Shall we call him Snowball?' Cait said, all flushed with excitement. 'I found the ewe rolling in the snow when I was bringing the horses down to the house for their rugs and hay.'

'We can't,' I said. 'He's black.'

'Yeah, I know, but he's rare like snow and black lambs can turn white when they grow up.'

'Hello, everybody, you all look like a nativity scene.' Maggie came in brushing snow off her jacket.

Spats followed and sniffed at Sean's trousers. He jumped back in case he was nipped again but the dog just went into his basket and licked his bottom.

When we finished our coffees Maggie told us to take her Land Rover in case the snow got thicker. Nuala changed her mind about visiting town and decided to stay at the farm to catch up with Maggie. Cait opted to stay with the lamb. I felt a bit guilty leaving her but I couldn't resist going and said I'd call in later.

# 12: THE NORWEGIANS

I sat between Dad and Sean on the front middle seat of Maggie's old Land Rover. Skidding slightly on the bends we made our way down the steep hill to Carran. Despite the freeze, high tide filled the harbour with lapping grey water. Lights from the Carran shops shone festively out of windows and doorways onto the snow-covered sea wall.

We parked outside The Atlantic and Dad clapped his hands to get attention. 'Shall we see how the chowder is today?' he asked.

A bowl of fish soup sounded great. I needed warming up after the drive down in Maggie's unheated Land Rover. The pub was crowded out with Saturday regulars and people who'd had their work stopped by the snow. A few farmers slurped pints at the bar, telling each other about the worst weather they'd ever seen.

I looked enviously at a family of visiting tourists whose children had baskets of chips in front of them. I started to tell Dad that I wanted chips but he was already halfway across the bar.

As soon as I saw them I knew that the four dishevelled men sitting round a long table under the window nursing little cups of espresso must be the Norwegian scientists.

Dad and Sean patted them on the backs. The men's faces lit up and they pulled their chairs back in an invitation for us to join them. I was very pleased to meet the intrepid Norwegians. I wanted to find out about their encounter with the seals. Dad asked them if they'd like chowder and they all declined emphatically.

'You should eat, it's the best cure for a hangover,' Sean said. Dad joined in trying to persuade them to eat and in the end they ordered four pints of Guinness and ham sandwiches.

'Well, I suppose Guinness is a hangover cure in itself.' Sean said he'd join them for the pint and would have the chowder. He sat down next to me, forcing me along to the centre of the table.

'Coke, Clare?' Dad asked. I felt so nervous about being surrounded by all the big men that I said yes even though I didn't really feel like a cold drink.

'So, you must be Liam's daughter, ja? I am Trigve.' The tallest, blondest Norwegian grinned at me appreciatively.

'Isn't she a lovely girl? She'll be a great help to us.' Sean spoke for me and I blushed, not knowing what to say next. I still wanted to ask them about the seals but didn't want to interrupt.

'Hello, my name is Leif.'

A shorter, dark-haired man wearing black-rimmed glasses and a traditional Norwegian jumper held out his hand.

Sean intervened again and introduced me to the men. 'Leif and Trigve, Ulf and Olaf.' He pointed at them all as he named them but I knew I'd never remember who was who apart from Trigve, the blond one, who was the friendliest by far. 'These are our herring experts from Trondheim University. We all help each other out when we can.'

Dad came back with a tray of drinks. 'Ah good, you've all met,' he said to us.

The Norwegians slurped their pints and the conversation turned to weather and the state of the tides. Chowder and sandwiches arrived and I soon felt warmed by the food. I liked being the only woman with all these attentive men. Sean was so funny and warm. He kept putting his arm around me whenever anyone spoke to me. I couldn't remember feeling happier for ages.

A blast of cold air cut across our conversation. The pub door opened, revealing a group of dark-coated people who'd been in the year above me at school. They were laughing and shaking snow out of their hair. I stiffened. The Kelly girls, who'd always seen me as an outsider, walked confidently over to the bar. Behind them, Joe Healey, who I knew because his parents were friends with mine, peeled away and stood chatting to someone by the window.

I wasn't sure whether to say hello or not and it took a few moments to notice that the man standing next to Joe was Ronan. He didn't look so awkward now with his collar turned up and a flush to his cheeks. He really wasn't the shy, boring boy I remembered. I couldn't believe I'd never noticed him before. I found, to my surprise, that I felt jealous thinking that he must have a girlfriend, which was weird as I didn't even think I liked him.

Sean grinned at me as he made a joke with Trigve and Dad about the nationality of herring. I turned back to our table. Here I was, in the company of Sean and four handsome Norwegians whose idea of fun was playing music to seals and surfing in the dark, even in the middle of winter. What was the lobsterman's sullen son compared to all that?

But I was drawn to the magnetic stillness of Ronan. I glanced back to see if he was looking over. He wasn't.

'Joe. How's it goin'? And how's your father?' Dad's voice cut across my reverie.

'He's grand, Liam, how are you?' Joe came over and stood behind me facing Dad.

'I wonder, do you know where he is? We're having a session tonight and it'd be great to have a bit of music.'

'He's not far behind us,' replied Joe. 'You can ask him yourself. Hello, Clare, you ok? Have you seen much of Cait? How is she?'

'Yeah, yeah, I'm fine. She's fine,' I mumbled. I liked Joe but felt very aware of Ronan and the Kellys standing behind him. At that moment, the door opened again. Joe's father, Martin Healey, and Martin's brother John spotted Dad and walked over.

'Martin, how are you? We're having a session up at the brewery tonight, would you come play for us? There'll be food and as much drink as you like.' Dad smiled encouragingly at the brothers and I really hoped they'd say yes.

'If Orla's there it'd be a great pleasure.' Joe's dad shook Dad's hand as he spoke, then asked after the family.

So it was settled that Martin with his accordion and John, the best concertina player for miles around, would be there with their wives, Bridie and Edie, who both played the fiddle. More drinks were offered, this time by the Norwegians who thought alcohol in Ireland so cheap compared to Norway that they were taking every opportunity to be generous to their hosts. Dad looked at his watch and declined the offer.

'Come and sit with us?' Ronan's soft voice shocked me from my thoughts. The Kellys and the two boys made their way to a separate table.

'Um, I think we're going in a minute.' As I spoke, I looked straight up into his eyes. The seal dream washed through my mind.

'Come up tonight, Ronan, and ask your father to bring his banjo,' my dad said.

A barmaid came to clear our plates and glasses away. The Norwegians stood up.

'We have to sleep before tonight I think,' explained Leif. 'We will walk. I don't think bicycles will work as well as skis in the snow.'

'I told you we should bring our skis,' added Trigve.

To my joy, Dad invited them all to come up before dark and to stay the night.

Outside it had stopped snowing and the street was quiet. Everybody must have been inside, out of the weather. Except for Ronan. There he was, standing with his back to the pub, rolling himself a cigarette.

'Will I see you tonight?' He didn't turn to me as he spoke but glanced at the sea, lapping at the harbour wall.

'Well yeah, but I might be at Cait's, she's a lamb to look after.' Then, catching myself, I added. 'But yeah, I'll be there, I'm sure.'

He blew out a long plume of cold smoke and shrugged. I suddenly wished more than anything that I could have stood with my back to the wall staring at the sea with him. As Dad walked out of the pub Ronan turned and muttered that he had to go. He nodded at Dad and walked away, pulling his hat out of his pocket as he did so.

At that moment Sean ran out. He ploughed to a standstill with a flourish and paused to catch his breath.

'Oh good, thank God you're still here. We were hoping you could take a load of beer up to the tower for us. Actually could I come back up with you now? I just need to pick up my clothes from the hostel,' he asked breathlessly.

'I don't see why I can't put you all in the back of the truck, you know,' Dad replied.

Forty minutes later the Land Rover, creaking with its load of beer and scientists, made its way back up the hill to the tower.

# 13: SLEDGING

Manic barking greeted the Land Rover when it crunched over the gravel drive and parked behind Mum's car. Dad got out to open the back for Trigve and the others. Then he asked me to take them to their sleeping quarters while he and Sean headed into the kitchen with bags of shopping and beer.

I showed the Norwegians to the circular room under the observatory. Dad must have banked up the stove before we went to town because it was lovely and warm in there. We disturbed the cats from their murderous dreams. They yawned, stretching tabby bellies on the sheepskin rugs before they ran away to hide as the men noisily chose a bed each to dump their bags on.

'We would love to visit your father's observatory. Can you show us, please?' Leif asked me very politely.

'No, first we should go out in the snow,' interrupted Trigve. He was a keen skier and had been pining for his snowy home.

'No, Trigve, you can play in the snow later. He just wants to show off, Clare. Now we must see the tower.' Leif laughed and squeezed Trigve's chin affectionately as though he was a child.

I climbed ahead of them and pushed open the trapdoor. It was great to have all these friendly men at our usually empty house.

The sky was heavy with snow and a pearly glow lit the crystal ceiling. Despite the fire in the room below, the observatory smelled cold, having been empty all day. I made a mental note to leave the hatch open. That way, if Cait and I ended up wanting to get away from the party, the observatory would be nice and warm. We'd got into the habit of making ourselves a den up under the dome, and had sleepovers there whenever the adults were having a session at the house.

The Norwegians rushed to the windows to look out at the view. I pointed out landmarks in the white landscape. White birches flared golden in the dying light as a pair of ravens flew over the tower. Echoes from the mountain replied to their raucous 'cronk cronks'. Looking up we could see the spread, glossy wingtips shining against a mauve sky.

'Ahoy up there,' Sean took the steps two at a time and arrived breathless at the top. I sat on a stool out of the way while he showed them my dad's equipment and maps.

'Ok, can we now walk in the snow?' Trigve urged his friends.

I waited at the top, watching them all clatter down the stairs. I was about to follow when Sean turned around and came up again.

'I just need to bring some papers down for Liam. Wait with me a minute and I'll show you what I need you to do for me.' He pointed to tables of numbers and symbols but it went over my head.

I breathed in the waxy smell of his coat, again remembering days out with my mum. How long ago that all seemed now.

'We need to record the numbers of birds with their ages, sex, date of arrival and so on. And we'll need numbers of breeding pairs and chicks, days they fledge, you get the picture.'

I nodded and tried to concentrate.

'You could be part of the team, helping collate the data and so on … send it back to the institute. Your dad said you were good at that sort of thing and I remember you had great fun re-organising your parents' library when I was here last.' He smiled briefly and went on: 'Fingers crossed, we're expecting a breeding population to establish on those sea-stacks we looked at. Maybe only one or two pairs, hopefully more.' His voice got faster. 'Last year, Clare, there were several males displaying to passing females. It's a kind of flirting. They're saying come and see the home I've found for you.'

All the time he was talking I could see his dimple appearing and disappearing and the creases round his eyes deepening as he smiled. He made earnest eye contact as he spoke about the gannets and I tried to look as interested as I possibly could. All I could think about was the difference between his joyous, easy interaction and the still silence of Ronan. If only it were Ronan in the tower with me instead, showing me stuff, eager to get his point across. How easily he would catch my mouth with his and I would let him kiss me.

'Hello!' Sean said. 'You still listening?'

I tried to say something useful. 'You know we don't have broadband here.' I could have kicked myself for saying that. I could have just done myself out of a job.

'But we are trying to get it and also we go all the time to the internet café in Carran.' Then I added, to press the point, 'Mum's really fed up not having it. So we'll definitely be getting it as soon as it reaches up the mountain. And it would make my dad's life a lot easier. He has to take all his work stuff to the café, too.'

'Ah well, that's rural living for you. Hey look, I can see your mum now.' Sean pointed out of the north window where a group of dark figures were walking up the slopes behind the house. Mum's red skirt and Nuala's pea green coat stood out from the men who were all wearing black, apart from Trigve whose white duvet jacket camouflaged him against the snow. The men carried what looked like pieces of black plastic.

'Come on, let's go and join them,' said Sean. 'Liam must have found something for sledging.' He grinned at me and stood back to allow my access to the stairs. As we walked down he told me a secret.

'Listen, darling girl. I've got to tell someone or else I'll burst.'

'What? What is it?' I asked.

He beamed at me, his eyes all sparkling and happy. 'There's something happening between Trigve and me. He likes me. Was it obvious in the pub?'

I hadn't noticed and I didn't even know Sean was gay. I racked my brains, searching for evidence of his gayness in years past. All I could think of was that there hadn't been any sign of a girlfriend. But then sometimes you don't see what you don't expect. I smiled back at him and hugged him.

'Wow! Sean, that's brilliant. He's lovely and plus it means I've got a proper gay friend. Sorry, is that offensive?'

'Not at all. Happy to oblige. Come on now, I'll keep you up to date with the gossip if you promise to tell me everything, and I mean anything, that anyone says about him.'

Cait was wrapped up for the snow. She looked like a four-year-old in her bright pink hat and gloves. Her cheeks and nose were red to match. She'd run almost all the way up the hill.

'Come on, everyone's sledging.' We ran ahead of Sean who went back towards the kitchen with his papers.

'Isn't he gorgeous?' Cait whispered.

'Apparently he's gay,' I replied.

'Oh my God, you're joking.'

'Yup, and he's in love with Trigve, but he told me not to tell.'

'Oh my God, that figures. I just met the Norwegians, Trigve does seem a bit gay. Actually they all seem a bit gay,' she added. 'Just our bloody luck.'

'No, Leif's got a wedding ring on, although ... that could mean anything. But the other two were definitely eyeing up the Kelly bitches. Come on, let's go sledging,' I laughed but suddenly wanted to cry. Thinking about the Kelly sisters had winded me. Somehow Ronan had got under my skin, what if he was dating one of them? The thought was more than I could bear.

# 14: BEFORE THE PARTY

After sledging Cait said she'd better go home to check Snowball and I, soaked from repeated falls off the black plastic 'sledges' that had no steering whatsoever, helped to clear up the broken pieces. Dad had made them from an old water butt, and the broken plastic lay in tatters looking like a massacre of crows.

Mum turned and waited for me to join her. Her dark hair was loose, obscuring half of her face. The grey beret pulled down over her forehead made her look like a freedom fighter. Her lipstick had faded but the brightness of her eyes had intensified. She held out gloved hands and hugged me.

'How's it with you, my lovely girl?' she said.

'Yeah, I'm fine.'

'I feel like we never really see each other. I wish you'd come to Dublin with me. Your granny's going to need me for another month at least. It's all been complicated by an infection. If I didn't have to be with her, I would be here with you, you know.'

'Yeah, I know Mum, but I'm all right here with Dad and I have revision classes that I can't really miss. And I'm going to help on the project. Sean says he'll properly pay me by the hour.'

'I'm so pleased he's back. He can be my stand-in.'

'Yeah, I suppose. But can't Auntie Chrissie stay a bit longer or take Granny back with her?'

'I don't know, Clare. Hopefully it won't be for too much longer. Anyway, tell me, are you going to wear the dress I got you tonight?'

Damn, I thought. I'd hoped Mum would have forgotten about the dress. I'd feel so much better in jeans. What would all those Norwegians think, seeing me dressed up like a doll? 'Mum, do you mind if I save it for a special occasion?'

'No, no of course not, I realise it's probably not your thing any more, is it? I'm sorry.'

'No Mum, it's … I love it. It's just that I think I'll be helping Cait with the lamb and I don't want to get it dirty. And there's the snow and everything.' I stared at my red hands, raw from having made snowballs without gloves. 'Do you need any help, only I said I'd go to get ready at Cait's and Maggie can bring us back later?'

'No, no, you go on and we'll see you when you're ready.' She hugged me again and then looked at me with fierce hawk-like intensity. 'I love you so much.' She pulled away and began a careful descent of the hill.

'Yeah, me too,' I replied.

'I'll take the dress back,' she shouted after me. 'You can have the money instead.'

I followed behind, watching her walk with arms spread out for balance. She usually seemed so strong but I suddenly saw her vulnerable and alone against the black trees. For the first time in my life I saw her as someone in her own right, rather than just my mother.

After going to my room for my clothes and make-up, I decided to grab something to eat from the kitchen before going down to Cait's. The house seemed very quiet. Everybody had vanished except for Dad who came dragging the log box in through the back door and Mum who stood at the dresser.

She had blood red splashes on her apron and around her mouth. Her hand held a small knife that was dripping a pool of scarlet stickiness onto the surface. She glanced up and smiled at me, baring reddened teeth. I wondered what on earth she was doing until I saw a cluster of disembowelled pomegranate skins. They'd been pushed into a heap behind a dark blue bowl that was brimming with shiny red seeds. She'd been licking the juice as she worked.

'Oh, hello love, you not gone to Cait's yet? These are for the meringues. I thought they'd look nice as … ' A single teardrop rolled down her cheek. Then her lips quivered as hot tears seeped from her eyes.

My dad stopped and looked at her with a perplexed frown on his face. I mumbled something about being late for Cait and abruptly left the kitchen.

As soon as I'd gone out into the hall I heard Dad's voice. He wasn't exactly shouting but he sounded cross. I didn't know what they were talking about but it was so rare to hear Dad raise his voice that I couldn't help standing there for a few moments.

'So who is he?' I heard him say. 'Every time I phone your mother's house she says you're out at the theatre or dinner. Is it with him?'

'He's just a friend!' she shouted back, and then she lowered her voice. 'Shush, there are people about.' Silence, and then in a pleading voice: 'I am entitled to go out while I'm there. I'd go mad stuck with Mum all day and night.'

I swallowed and stood on the bottom stair. Then I heard something truly terrible. It was the sound of my dad crying. The strangled choke of someone not used to crying. That was it. I was off. I ran down the hill to Cait's and on the way there I replayed the scene again and again. Mum, Dad. My mum and a man? The theatre. Dad crying. Mum … ? And I couldn't decide whether or not to tell Cait. I think I felt ashamed. What sort of a family were we?

By the time I got to the farm it was nearly time to come back again. Cait looked gorgeous, in a silky emerald green top. I had hardly any time to get ready and didn't feel like getting dressed up, anyway. Maggie drove us up with some puddings and asked me to tell Dad and Mum she'd be back when she'd checked her ewes.

We walked around to the kitchen door, carrying a trifle and an apple pie for the party. I cautiously opened the door hoping the kitchen would be empty. It wasn't. Mum and Dad were still there. They were sitting in silence, she holding his hands, both of them looking down. I saw reflected light circles bouncing off their wine glasses and overlapping on the table. The circles looked like a geometry question from my maths revision book. They sprang apart and stood up.

'Oh God, Clare, Cait. What time is it?' Mum's face was still stained from the pomegranates and you could tell she'd been crying. I glanced at Cait, hoping she hadn't noticed.

Dad disappeared out into the night saying he had to walk the dogs. Mum retied her apron and pulled her hair into a knot. Then, thank God, Nuala walked in.

Nuala always made everything normal again. I could remember times in my childhood when Mum's tears would turn to shrieks of laughter after a few minutes with her.

Mum lit candles all along the windowsill then suddenly turned around. 'Shit!' She threw open the oven door.

A smell of burnt sugar filled the room. The meringue for her Pavlova was a black wafer. She'd never got to grips with cooking in a solid fuel range. Mum, who was renowned for her wonderful desserts, still always forgot how hot the range could be when it had been on all day. One moment it was too cold, the next it was a blast furnace.

'Bugger it. I should have put it in the slow oven first thing.' She started crying again, only this time it wasn't a few demure tears but a torrent of sobbing.

'Come here, Orla, love.' Nuala wrapped her strong arms around Mum, who seemed to have shrunk into a dishevelled little bird.

'Come on now, we'll go and get you spruced up.' She looked over Mum's shoulder at me. 'Clare love, would you sort out glasses and plates, you know the sort of thing.'

'Get the … ' Mum started to mumble instructions through her choking sobs but Nuala shushed her and drew her away.

'Clare's perfectly capable now. Let's leave her to it.'

'I'll be fine, Mum.' I knew my way around the kitchen better than her, anyway. She seemed to have forgotten so much about our lives lately.

Cait and I set about making the kitchen look festive. I felt strangely elated. Though it had been a horrible shock to see my parents crying, I felt reassured that they were still capable of talking and holding hands. I'd known there was something wrong but I felt certain they'd sort things out. They had to, didn't they? They always had before.

We found glasses and crockery and a packet of Christmas napkins that were perfect as they were black with silver snowflakes on them.

'We'll have to wait for them to tell us about the wine,' I said. 'Hey, let's have some now.' I picked up my parents' discarded bottle and, even though I knew it was wrong, a little surge of anger made me throw it with a loud smash into the re-cycling bin outside the back door. Dad would go mad when he found the broken glass.

Sensing that nobody would notice or care I pulled open the pantry door and with a triumphant flourish presented Cait a bottle of white wine and some crisps. We set about sipping and giggling once more about Sean and Trigve. I tried to push thoughts of Mum and Dad to the very back of my mind. Luckily Cait didn't ask any questions.

# 15: MUSICIANS

We heard a car and ran outside to see who had come. Nightfall had brought a freeze with it and the snow had turned to ice. Donal's Range Rover skidded onto the gravel. We stood waiting with Dad while the dogs pirouetted and barked around the visitors.

Donal got out, leaving the Healey brothers with wives on their knees squashed into the back seat. The boot was full of fishing gear so Donal had packed the instruments into the front seat and foot well. The accordion and John's concertina sat on the floor with a crate of beer wedged between them. A flute case and two fiddles dovetailed into the body of a mandolin. Rearing up behind the handbrake all the way back to the roof above Bridie's head was Donal's banjo.

Everybody looked a bit bent from accommodating the vulnerable instrument in its long black case. The doors opened and creaking knees emerged followed by the jolly crowd dressed in their glad rags and ready for a session. Dad leant in and took the mandolin from Edie.

'Are the boys coming up?' he asked Donal.

'Ah well, they might, you know, Joe's working on the bar till nine, but he can borrow the pub van later and he knows Ronan's invited.'

Dad led them into the sitting room behind the kitchen and invited everyone to leave their instruments and coats on the old orange velvet sofa. We never used that room and though the fire had been going all day there was a lingering musty damp smell in there. Dad asked me to go up and tell Mum that the guests had arrived so, leaving Cait to hand out drinks, I went along to my parents' bedroom, hoping that Nuala would have calmed Mum down.

Mum was standing by the window brushing her hair in the reflection. Beyond the black glass, moonlight lit the frozen snow making the birch trunks glitter. Her hands shook as she tried to tie her hair up into a knot.

'Love, let me do that.' Nuala got up from sitting on the bed and I could see the reflection in the glass as Nuala twisted the wild coils into a taming silver and pearl clasp. 'You look great.' Nuala stood back to admire. She smiled at me. 'Isn't she lovely, Clare?'

Mum had dressed in black. The red dress she'd planned to wear was lying crumpled on the floor. My mother seemed to be in mourning.

'Clare,' Mum said and then sat on the bed and patted it. 'Come and sit with me, love.'

I started to tell her that the guests had arrived but stopped when I saw yet more tears rolling down her face. Her perfect eye make-up was running in black streaks over her cheekbones. She turned her tearstained face towards me.

'I think it would suit you to study in Dublin next year.' Mum stood up and walked back towards the window. 'God, I hate this place,' she groaned.

I didn't know what to say and stood looking at the floor and the crumpled red dress. Evidence of plans gone awry.

'Come to Trinity,' she said it as though she lived there now. 'And do literature or history. You don't have to do science. You don't have to follow your father.' She stared out at the mountain and then turned, holding out her hands like someone drowning, bobbing and reaching out for rescue.

Nuala took her outstretched hand. 'Orla, love, Clare might think of having a gap year. Let her take her time. She's a great opportunity here, working with Sean.'

Nuala winked at me as though to tell me that this would all blow over. Mum sighed and looked at us both.

'Help me sort this out, would you?' She pointed at her face and we all laughed.

A quiet tap on the door made us jump. Dad put his head round the door. 'I've to change if you don't mind. We've guests Orla,' he added pointedly. 'The Healeys and Donal are here.'

A sudden gust of wind threw handfuls of ice at the windowpanes. He walked over to pull the curtains shut and turned to Nuala and me.

'Go on down. We won't be long.'

Nuala took my arm and squeezed it tightly to her side.

# 16: THE PARTY

We got back to the kitchen to find Donal and the Healeys sitting at the table. The men swigged beer from bottles while the women sipped whiskey from tumblers. Opened wine bottles were breathing on the shelf next to the range and little dishes of olives and things sat alongside Mum's breads. A foil wrapper of crab, which Donal had contributed to the gathering, leaked its fishy smell through the general fug.

I walked over to the sink with Cait, listening to everyone say hello to Nuala and was relieved when Mum and Dad came in. Mum looked restored and carried off her role of perfect hostess with ease. She beamed at everybody and the men stood to greet her.

'It is great to see you, Orla.' John Healey took her hand and hugged her.

My mum was the kind of woman who made people feel special. She always took time to ask important questions about a person's life. She really did care and that came across. All the people in the kitchen had had reason to take my mum into their confidence at one time or another. You could tell that they all found her warm, funny and engaging. When she looked at people with her knowing hazel eyes they felt attractive and important. It was a gift she had, making you feel important. I was proud of the way she did that.

Mum looked gratefully at John. She hugged everybody, including me, then asked me to fetch the champagne.

'Let's get this party started,' she said, her eyes bright as she took the cold wet bottle from me. As the cork popped into her hand the back door opened.

'Ah ha! We have arrived in time.' Trigve was swept in by the force of an icy gust of wind and the other Norwegians pushing behind him. Beaming and ruddy-faced, they pulled off their ski hats to reveal crazy ruffled hair. The four men seemed huge and filled the kitchen with their animal bulk. Dad reached behind Leif and pulled the door shut.

'Put your coats next door, lads, and we'll find you a drink.' He nodded to Cait and me. We jumped up and showed them into the living room.

'We should have brought our didgeridoo.' Trigve saw all the instruments on the sofas and looked crestfallen. 'Never mind, we can sing.' Leif thumped him on the back and sang an out of tune scale.

Mum filled glasses with champagne and we brought more chairs in to squeeze everybody around the big table.

'Where is Sean?' Trigve asked, looking at nobody in particular. The other Norwegians began making whooping sounds and nudged him. He grinned, seeming not to care what anyone thought.

'I will go and find him.'

Trigve tried to get up from the table, causing several people's drinks to splash onto it. He sat down and then tried again, this time being careful not to knock against it. He moved in an ungainly humped posture, pushing his chair back with his knees. He thanked Dad for the bottle of beer that had been thrust into his hand and turned to leave. At that moment Sean walked in, pushing the door into Trigve so that the bottle crashed into his teeth. The other Norwegians laughed loudly. They obviously thought of Trigve as their pet clown.

'Shut up, you guys,' he frowned, and then shouted 'Skol!' and raised his bottle up to the ceiling. I thought he looked like a real Viking with his wayward blond hair and three days of straw-like stubble. His jumper had a polar bear design that bore the legend ISBJORN in black woollen letters. I couldn't help imagining his bearlike arms around little Sean.

'Where's your mother?' Bridie asked Cait.

'I thought she'd be here by now. Will I ring her?'

'Go on, do,' Dad said, handing her the phone. 'She's missing the champagne.'

# 17: MCGUAN'S RAMS

Cait rang the number and we all waited.

'There's no answer.' She put the phone back on its cradle and looked at Dad.

'She must be on her way so.' Dad clapped his hands. 'Beer, lads!' he said to the Norwegians.

Dad had his new jacket on, and his face was shiny from shaving. I noticed he was wearing aftershave. It smelled unusual on Dad, who scorned such things. I wondered where he'd got it, and felt sad to see him trying so hard.

Nuala looked at Cait. 'Have you tried her mobile?'

'There's no point. We can't get a signal at the house. You've to walk halfway to Carran to get one.' This was a constant source of frustration to us. Whilst our classmates spent hours every day texting each other and going onto Facebook with their broadband connections, we were stuck in the dark ages with no mobile phone signal and no Internet.

A loud ring made me jump. Dad picked up the phone, listened for a while and then put the phone down.

'That was Maggie,' he said. 'McGuan's rams must have got to more of her sheep. She's up to her neck in birthing ewes.' He looked apologetically at the Healeys.

'I'll have to go and help.'

'Sure, we'll all come and help.' John Healey stood up. He was a farmer himself and, like all farmers, was happy to help a friend in need.

'God I wouldn't dream of it, John. You're on a night off. You'll be lambing yourself in a week or so. Anyway, we'll need music later when we come back.' Dad took off his smart jacket and went out to the hall to change his boots.

Donal went out to offer Dad a lift down in the Range Rover. He accepted the offer and the two men left the house.

I held on to the dogs' collars. 'You can't go, you'll frighten the sheep.' I pushed them down into their beds.

'Will I put the crab out now?' I asked Mum.

'Here love, you sit down. Let me do all that. Sure you wouldn't know how to lay it out.' Bridie Healey got up from her seat. She was from a fishing family and had cooked the seafood herself. Though she'd married a farmer, she and Donal ran a stall selling fish and seafood on the quay. Mum had told me she'd been a great comfort to Donal when his wife died. Bridie was very fond of Ronan and thought of him as an extra son. I'd always found her a bit fierce. We all watched her crack the crab claws and fish out the flesh.

'Will you give me an onion, love?' She looked at Cait who was still standing by the back door.

Bridie chopped it finely, and added it with lemon juice to the crabmeat. Then she piled it into one of Mum's black clay bowls and put it in the centre of the table. She broke the rest of the crabs into pieces and arranged them on a board for people to help themselves. She said she thought the Norwegians would enjoy the primitive delight of pulling them apart and sucking out the flesh.

Cait and I, tired of adult conversation, decided to walk down to see how the lambing was going. What we really wanted to do was go the long way down to the lake along the main road, hoping that the boys from Carran might come along. On the way down she told me how much she liked Joe Healey and I found myself talking about Ronan.

'But he's so weird.' Cait said. 'Don't you remember how he never had friends at school? All the boys thought he was a dick.'

'You just don't know him,' I countered. 'If you'd seen him that day on the boat and on the island, he seemed different. And he's really hot. I think we've just never seen him properly before.' I picked up a handful of snow and squashed it smooth as a pebble.

'I suppose I haven't ever seen him do anything except look embarrassed and stand behind other people. How did his mother die, I wonder?' Cait made an ice pebble, too, and we threw them into the snow.

'Why can't you and my brother get together? Then we'd be related for-ever.' Cait laughed and put her arm in mine.

'Yeah, my mum always says that. I do love your brother, but like a brother. Anyway I'm sure he's met someone at college by now.'

'Not according to Mum. He still really likes you, you know.'

I felt embarrassed again. The last thing I wanted to do was hurt Tom or Cait or Maggie or anybody, come to that. But the thought of kissing Tom just didn't work for me.

'I had a dream about Ronan. He was a seal in my dream and he made me feel like one, too. I think he's got eyes like a seal.'

Cait laughed. 'Maybe he's a selkie and he's come to lure you away into the sea. Maybe that's what happened to his mum and she went back to her people. Actually, I think my mum said she did drown, come to think of it.'

'Hah-hah.' I said. 'You don't really believe in the seal people now.'

'My mum says that the myth of seals becoming human and letting peo-ple fall in love with them is a metaphor for us following our soul's dreams,' said Cait. 'Whatever.'

'They're usually women, aren't they?' I asked. 'The selkies.'

'No, they can be men as well,' Cait said.

'Well, maybe Ronan is my soul's dream. Anyway, I wouldn't mind fol-lowing him into the sea. You should see him with his coat off. He's really fit.'

Ever watchful of the road, we made our way down the hill towards the farm.

# 18: THE LAMBING SHED

Bright snow illuminated the dark hulk of the lambing shed. We could hear Spats barking in the kitchen and peered in through the window. Remnants of food preparation littered the table along with Maggie's handbag and keys. We went in and peeped into Snowball's box by the stove. Considering how much racket Spats had made it was surprising that the lamb should be asleep. We decided to let him be and went to see the lambing.

Cracks in the walls showed light from within the old barn. The hinges creaked as we pushed open the stiff door. Maggie, on all fours, leaned over a collapsed ewe. In a makeshift pen to her left, two more ewes attended to their black-faced twins. One licked a sleepy new-born. The other stood while robust twin lambs nudged her udders, looking for milk.

Donal and my dad crouched on the other side of the ewe. Maggie looked up at us, hair falling over her face. Sitting back on her haunches she pulled her gloves off and tied her hair back into a lopsided ponytail.

'I'm positive she's having a big singleton. It's stuck. I can feel one foot but I can't seem to get to the other one,' she said.

'Do you want me to have a go or shall we get the vet?' Dad put his hand onto the ewe's heaving flanks.

'I think it might be too late for the vet. We've been here a while. You have a go.'

Dad didn't bother looking for gloves but slipped his hand into the ewe and tried to feel for the lamb's hooves. She must have progressed since Maggie's last attempt because he said: 'Got them,' as the hooves slid into his probing hand.

'There's something wrong, Maggie,' he said. 'There's no pulse in the feet and they aren't very warm.'

She looked crestfallen until he added: 'Tell me when you think she might be contracting and I'll give it all I can.'

I could see Dad bracing himself as he waited for Maggie's signal. 'It's a big lamb,' he grunted. 'I can see why she hasn't been able to push it out. It's stuck solid.' He frowned and Cait and I held on to each other, terrified at what might happen next. We could see its feet, though, which gave me some hope.

'Here, you pull from outside and I'll get my hand in to encourage it along.' As Maggie's hand was smaller than his she was able to reach in and ease the lamb into position. Her face flushed as she strained to help the ewe, which groaned and tried to get to her feet. Suddenly in a rush of blood and waters the big lamb slid onto the straw. It lay perfectly still.

'I'm sorry, Maggie.' Dad said as he patted the little body.

Though the lamb's lips were blue, we did see a flicker of movement in its tightly closed mouth. And then Donal bent down over its slippery head and blew softly into its mouth while Dad rubbed it with straw. The lamb's chest rose and fell in time with Donal's breathing and after what seemed like forever a hind leg suddenly twitched and its body shuddered.

'Oh God, Donal. You've done it.'

Dad vigorously rubbed the lamb while Maggie checked the ewe. The afterbirth slid onto the floor beside them and the ewe sighed a huge sigh.

Dad and Donal high fived each other, which I thought was uncharacteristic of both of them but appreciated the sentiment.

'I've had a thought,' Maggie said, looking at Cait and me. 'If we rub Snowball with the afterbirth this ewe may accept him as her own. Girls, would you go and fetch him? We'll give it a go.'

We didn't need asking twice and ran to the kitchen. Cait let me pick up Snowball's warm, sleepy body. He felt full of vitality as he struggled against my embrace.

Spats followed but sat quietly by the lambing shed door. He knew better than to disturb his mistress. Dad rubbed Snowball with the afterbirth. He said he wished he'd worn gloves.

The ewe was full of milk-yielding hormones and barely registered the interloper on her teat. Before long the little black lamb was suckling next to the white one twice his size. Both lambs' tails were wagging frantically.

# 19: THE BOYS ARRIVE

We arrived back at the tower to find the pub van parked up in the drive. As we got out of Donal's car, the van door opened and Joe Healey got out. I squeezed Cait's hand and tried not to grin.

'Hello, folks, we made it.'

He seemed to be alone until he opened the back doors and Ronan stepped out and handed a crate of beer to Joe.

'We've found some Biddle's in the pub cellar. I thought your dad might like it.' Ronan looked briefly at me.

'It might be off by now but hey, let's give it a go,' Joe said, and smiled at Cait.

'We've brought some sleeping bags, we can sleep in the van,' he added.

'No. It's too cold. We'll find room for you,' I said, thrilled that they were planning to stay. 'We can all sleep in the tower.'

'Yeah, that'd be really cool,' agreed Cait. The boys didn't protest.

Joe picked up the beer and we all made our way into the kitchen, crunching frozen leaves that had been lying there since the autumn.

Mum stood to greet the boys. 'We've saved a bit of food but you'd better be quick about it.' She kissed Joe, and then stood back whilst Bridie brought plates to the table for them. 'Come on girls, you've not eaten much either.' Mum glanced at me.

'You are lucky we didn't eat all the crab, it is very good.' Trigve touched my shoulder and pulled a chair out for me. The other Norwegians rose to make space for Cait and the boys. Maggie shuffled along mid-forkful. She must have been starving after her long day.

'The room next door should be warm now.' Dad had changed and turned from a sheep farmer back into a host. The Healeys went ahead and began tuning their instruments. Donal showed Dad the case of Biddle's.

'Look at this, Liam, the lads found it in The Atlantic's cellar. Vintage Biddle's.'

Dad clapped his hands and opened a few bottles of the dark beer.

'Paddy Biddle, God rest his soul.' He raised the bottle and the other men echoed his gesture. 'Paddy Biddle.' Together they drank deeply and smacked their lips with appreciation.

Trigve interrupted. 'Mighty herring, king of the sea,' he said, clinking his bottle to Leif's.

Donal countered that with a toast to the Irish mackerel. After that there were several more toasts to lobsters, crabs, Maggie and her sheep, McGuan and his rams, Dad and Donal for saving the day and so on and so on.

'Well, they don't make beer like that anymore, do they?' Dad said.

'No, the Guinness is probably imported from China nowadays.' Donal agreed. 'Do you remember when it took half the day for a good pint to settle? Now it comes frozen out of a tap, all homogenised.'

Cait and I caught each other's glance. This could be a long conversation. Next door, thankfully, Bridie and Edie lifted their violins and began playing a reel together. We all went in to watch. Before long John had his hands round his little concertina and Martin had the accordion stretched out. I sat by the door and listened whilst the four musicians flowed effortlessly together into a haunting rendition of 'Port na bPucai'. The beautiful tune, written for the sound of whales singing in Blasket Sound, drew the crowds. Everyone crammed themselves into the room except for Joe, Ronan and Mum who stayed behind. After a few minutes, Cait and I went back to join them.

Wafts of fiddle music drifted into the steamed up kitchen. As Mum busied herself around the sink, piling plates and dropping cutlery into a bowl of soapy water, I found myself watching her back at the sink and had to look away when she suddenly turned. When her eyes met mine I could tell that she knew I had overheard her argument with Dad. I had to get my friends out of there.

'Mum, we're going up to the tower, is that ok?' I knew she wouldn't say no.

'Of course it is, love, and take some food if you want. I'll see you later.' With that Mum picked up a bottle of wine and went in to join the others in the living room. I glanced in to wave goodbye. She sat in the corner under the window and gazed dreamily at Bridie's bow as it wove in and out through the music. I saw Edie catch her eye and glance down at the flute she'd brought along. Though Mum did play, she was normally too shy to join such accomplished musicians as the Healeys. But something inside her tonight must have made her brave.

The firelight suited her tearstained face, concealing any red blotches. Her long fingers slid over the silver keys and she placed her mouth to the flute. Her bass notes blended with the soulful violins and her high notes filled the room with birdsong. She'd her eyes closed, away with the music. Time seemed static as everyone entered an ancient frame of mind. The warmth of good company and a crackling fire, candlelight dancing off the glowing faces, the music and the laughter—maybe Nuala was right. Everything would be ok.

Back in the kitchen, Cait was stuffing bottles of beer into two big shopping bags.

'Are you sure we can take all this?' she asked.

'They're too pissed to notice anything now and anyway, who cares?'

I went to the fridge and took out a bottle of champagne. 'Let's go,' I said, getting excited about our private party plans.

I could smell Ronan; a mixture of turf smoke from the pub and the fishy, diesel boat smell that permeated all his coats and boots. His eyes betrayed no expression but he stood close to me and offered to carry the bags. Outside the back door a blast of wind surprised us, nearly blowing us over.

'Where the fuck did that come from?' Ronan said. The northern freeze was being chased away by a warm southwesterly gale.

'Oh no, the snow will melt.'

We were disappointed. Sure enough, a million drips from thawing trees serenaded us as we made past the front of the house towards the tower.

Inside the living room the temperature must have risen. Long streams of condensation glittered down the windows. The ebb and flow of the music seemed to be calling up the wind.

Cait, energetic as ever, was determined to make the most of the snow.

'Hey, let's make a snowman before it all goes,' she shouted.

'The rain will wash it away,' Joe argued.

Minute by minute, a strong smell of the sea was clearing away the arctic atmosphere and turning the fairy kingdom back into its everyday self.

'If we make one big enough, it'll last all night,' pleaded Cait.

'Yeah, and it'd cheer Trigve up if we saved him a bit of snow,' I said.

'Trigve's other things on his mind,' whispered Cait.

Ronan gathered armfuls of snow and had constructed a base in no time. Together we rolled a giant snowball.

'Hey, let's make it into a snow seal.' My flash of inspiration had come from my dream, or was it from the proximity of Ronan? They all thought it was a good idea and we honed it with great attention to detail. Joe pushed two empty beer bottles into the seal's head to form dark shiny eyes. The claws and mouth were birch twigs and we made the nose with an inverted pinecone. Snow melt and rain drops were already pitting the seal's back but that didn't stop us finishing our creation.

'What'll we call him?' Joe asked.

'I think it's a her,' I said. None of us could think of a name but we did all agree that the seal was sleek enough to be a female.

Joe took Ronan up to see the tower while Cait and I went into the room below.

'I'll stoke the fire, you get the blankets,' I said. 'They're in that cupboard.'

She suddenly gripped my arm in excitement. 'Oh my God, Clare, I think I'm in love.'

'When he looks at me.' Her eyes glittered as she squeaked triumphantly. 'I know he likes me ... and I've liked him for ages, but I've only just realised it. He is the one.'

She jumped up and down, looking possessed or drunk or mad. 'He put his arm round me when we were outside.' She grinned at me and whispered: 'If he really wanted to ... you know ... I think I'd do it.' She looked defiant, as though expecting me to argue with her.

'We've known each other all our lives. It's all just clicked in my head. Do you know what I mean?'

I might have been shocked a week earlier but now I knew exactly what she meant.

'But what about ...? Really, would you really do it?' I stammered.

'I just hope he's got a condom because I haven't. Have you?'

'No, no I haven't, but anyway don't, Cait. He might do it all the time with everyone and he might not know it's your first time. Be cool.'

I was suddenly afraid for my friend. It was one thing having gorgeous dreams about falling into somebody's arms but to really do that with some-one, well, that was a whole new world for both of us. I was impressed and jealous and slightly horrified all at the same time. I couldn't yet imagine being with Ronan in that way. I'd never even seen a man naked before and couldn't quite imagine how it would be to see him, or for him to see me. The desire I felt was replaced by waves of anxiety and I envied Cait's easy excitement.

Joe had seen the tower before but Ronan hadn't ever been up to the house. We laid out the blankets while he walked from window to window exclaiming at the views. Together we lit a clutch of Mum's tea-lights, and once we'd settled in our woolly nest I set up a row of Dad's whiskey glasses and popped open the champagne bottle.

We didn't toast anything but the fizzing wine made us smile and we sat together talking and laughing until our long day caught up with us. Despite my excitement about being so close to Ronan, I must have fallen asleep because sometime in the middle of the night I was aware of the Norwegians stumbling into the room underneath us. The candles had burned down and we were lying in a heap, snuggled close for warmth like a pile of puppies. We were fully clothed but with arms and legs entwined. Ronan had his head nestled into my neck.

# 20: AFTER THE PARTY

In the morning I woke myself up, choking for air and dislodging my head from Ronan's armpit, I lay on my back staring up at the dome where rain cascaded over its curves. Following the drops as they ran down the glass, I tried to remember my dream.

*The snow seal slithers away down the hill towards the lake. She slides into the water where another seal is waiting. They disappear under the water and I feel myself suffocating.*

The cosy feeling of being so close to Ronan was eclipsed by the dream. I think the seal in the dream might have been my mother. Ronan rolled away from me with a long sigh and I moved around him, breathing into his neck. I replayed how we'd come up to the tower with our sheepskins and curled around each other.

Cait hadn't been shy with Joe and I'd tried not to notice them kissing and giggling. Ronan didn't kiss me and I was too timid to approach him, but we'd lain on our backs and traced the glass frieze above with pointing fingers. The flickering candlelight had brought it to life and while ignoring Joe and Cait's muffled giggles I'd revelled in the quiet presence of the dark man beside me.

He must have heard my thoughts because he stirred and rolled towards me. He looked at me without speaking. We let ourselves be looked at. I saw into the bottomless depths of his sea-green eyes and removed all defences from my own. I felt myself falling down to the seabed, then swimming up to the surface and breathing properly for the first time in my life. I'd never been in love before. In that moment I felt it. A pain that meant I'd never feel complete again.

It was the beginning of something but also the end. Now I knew I would care less for my true needs and more for how to reclaim this feeling of falling. All at once I wanted to be in him, to be part of him. I'd never had sex with anybody but I understood now that it was nothing to do with that physical ache. It was this need to merge with another. I couldn't tear my eyes away.

'You've got me.' I stated the true fact to him. Said it out loud.

He didn't speak but he pulled me close so that our bodies pressed together. He didn't kiss me or fumble with my clothes. He didn't writhe or groan or talk. He simply held me and let me be aware of his desire. I kept perfectly still, trying to listen to the silent conversation of our bodies. It was the simplest and most effective of foreplays. I couldn't contain myself. I pushed him back and crouched over him.

'Please do it to me,' I whispered, surprising myself with the fierceness of my voice. He didn't speak, just sat himself up and gently pushed me away. I couldn't believe it. I'd never offered myself to a boy before. Why would he refuse? I turned away, hot with confusion and tried to pretend I'd never spoken. The important thing now was to stop him leaving.

'Hey, let's go in and get some breakfast,' I pulled at Cait who was wrapped in Joe's embrace. She opened her sleepy eyes and grinned at me. Straightaway I realised that those two had not been so chaste. I was very envious. Joe was a sexy, funny, confident boy, and probably a great lover. My friend had beaten me to it.

Why did I have to fall for someone quiet and complicated like Ronan? He stood up and stilled my fears by taking my hand in his. I followed him down the stairs. We peeped into the Norwegian's room and saw three men, fully dressed and snoring away on top of their blankets. I noticed Trigve's absence and was happy for Sean.

I led Ronan into the kitchen where Dad sat at the table with Nuala. Sean and Trigve stood warming themselves by the range. Sean wore an old dressing gown of Dad's and Trigve sported the tiniest towel tucked around his loins. As we came in Sean nodded at me and, cradling coffee cups, he and Trigve retired to wherever they'd come from.

'Sit down, love,' Nuala said to me. 'And you, Ronan, let me get you coffee, or is it tea you'd prefer?' She bustled cheerfully to the sink and clattered about with cups. 'Shame the snow's all gone,' she said. 'Trigve was most put out.'

As Nuala chatted away, my dad was silently sitting with his head in his hands. I was surprised that he hadn't challenged me about where we had all slept. I had all the answers ready.

'Where's Mum?' I asked them, to steer the conversation well away from that.

'Clare, love, listen,' Nuala said. 'Your mother has had to go back to Dublin. She left with Gerry and Jeanette early this morning.'

I looked at Dad. 'Is it because of Granny?'

I knew it wasn't

'That's part of it, love.' I could hear her trying to cover up for Mum and then she couldn't lie to me. 'Your mother just needs a little time on her own.'

There it was. I knew it all along. She was leaving us and not coming back. Ronan stared at the table, well out of his comfort zone and suddenly I couldn't be bothered with any of it.

'Come on,' I said. 'Let's go and find the others.'

As we walked back to the tower Ronan took my hand in his, causing my stomach to lurch in a mixture of dread and anticipation. But then he kissed me and all thought left my head. Nothing mattered now except that I needed him and wanted him and would do anything to have him.

# Part Two
## BROODING AND HATCHING

# 21: WIND AND RAIN

Cait, Joe and I walked back from school together on a damp morning in early April. Low cloud concealed the mountains and mist shrouded the dripping forests. The rain was fine, the sort that gradually soaked you through before you noticed. We trudged up the hill, heads bent, Joe and Cait holding hands. Tom was home and Cait had spent most of the walk telling me that I had to come and say hello.

'You've got to, he's dying to see you.'

It was a nice idea, to sit round Maggie's warm table and delay the uphill walk home, so I said yes.

We found Tom standing at the door looking out at the rain.

'Dude!' he said to Joe, punching him on the arm. 'Hey Sis, Mum said to tell you to hay the horses before you come in.'

Cait pushed him out of the way. 'They're ok. I fed them this morning, they won't need hay till later.'

We peeled off our wet coats and sat around the table. Tom smiled at me and I smiled back but wished he'd stop just grinning at me without saying anything. He was definitely more attractive these days, especially since he'd been away to college, but of course I could only think of Ronan. Cait was always going on about how she thought Ronan was weird and that her brother was a great catch. It was beginning to make me not want to tell her anything. I'd found my catch.

I drank Tom's tea before leaving the warm kitchen to walk home. The rain had eased to a general dampness and it was so warm and muggy that little clouds of midges appeared over the ferns and I ran to get past them. When I eventually reached the drive I saw Donal's car.

My heart jumped at the thought that maybe Ronan had borrowed it to visit me. But it was only Sean at the wheel.

'Hello, Clare,' he said. 'Sit in here out of the wet.'

He was looking very pleased with himself and said he had a treat in store for me. Donal had told him that the next day looked likely for a trip out to the island, as the wind would be light. He asked if I'd like to join him on a visit to the gannet site.

'We'll have to leave early, mind, to tie in with Donal checking his pots. He's lobster fishing now so it's always an early start. We'll try to persuade Liam to come and he'll give you a lift down.'

I felt surge after surge of adrenaline. There was no way I wouldn't bump into Ronan. He was bound to be working full time with Donal now that the lobster season had started. I hadn't seen either him or my mum since the morning after the party. And although I spoke to Mum on the phone every night, I hadn't seen or heard from Ronan for almost four weeks. It was doing my head in.

I'd thought of writing a letter to give to Sean for him, but no matter how I phrased things the letters always sounded so pathetic and needy that I screwed them into balls and burnt them in the range.

I couldn't believe that our night hadn't meant as much to him. But maybe I'd been too intense and frightened him. My worst fear was that he would never want to see me again. But then I'd think it must be because he was too busy with fishing or that he was too shy to make another move.

Perhaps he was waiting for me to contact him. I went round and round it every day, driving myself crazy and feeling hopelessly and painfully in love with an illusion.

Sean said he was coming in to see Dad. As we crunched over the gravel towards the tower Maggie came out of the kitchen door.

'Sean, Clare, I'm just off, tell Liam there's a casserole in the oven and I've done the kitchen and bathrooms.'

Mum had persuaded Dad to take on Maggie as a cleaner until she came home from Dublin. It was a huge relief to me. I was far too busy with my emotional turmoil to cope with Dad nagging me about cleaning.

'Is Cait home, Clare?' she added. 'I hope she's not brought Joe with her again. She really needs to get down to her work.'

I didn't say anything except 'She is home,' but I gave her a shrug to let her know that Joe was indeed there.

Sean followed me up to the dome where my dad sat, engrossed in tide tables and nautical maps. The rain had started again, hammering the glass and obscuring the views.

'Sean,' he said, getting off his stool and holding a hand out in welcome.

'We were beginning to think you'd left the country, Liam. You don't come down to The Atlantic any more.'

Dad glanced at me and said in a low voice: 'Clare's mother's not back yet. I'm holding the fort.'

'What fort?' I said

Sean smirked, Dad scowled but then he brightened and changed the subject: 'So, how are the lads?'

'They've gone home for Easter, they'll be back in May.' He paused and added: 'And Trigve's left me for a polar bear project on Svalbard. It was a no-brainer, he's the film man; it'll make his career. Oh Clare, by the way, there are plenty of seals on the island and a group of dolphins are hanging about by the stacks waiting for the fish.'

He looked back at Dad: 'Liam; you really should come down to the café. The Norwegian lads have set up a link for us with their own herring people. They're giving us news about the stocks up there and they've contacts all the way down to southern Portugal. You'll come with us anyway, won't you, to the island tomorrow? Donal's expecting us.'

Dad pushed his books to one side and said he might.

I went to bed full of hopes and fears. Eventually, I fell asleep and dreamed about Ronan.

*He's lying in the surf, bobbing backwards and forwards with the waves. He looks dead the way he lets the sea pull him about. As I lean over him he opens his eyes and stretches his arms up to pull me down onto the wet sand. I resist at first, but then my legs give way and I'm face down in the water. I can't breathe and I panic.*

A paralysing terror woke me and I found myself unable to open my eyes or move. After a few minutes I woke fully and rekindled in my mind the lovely moments in the tower when we'd cuddled together. Then I groaned and turned over. Why had he disappeared? Why hadn't he tried to contact me?

# 22: THE OLD COTTAGE

It was a warm damp morning in Carran. I felt uncomfortable in my water-proofs and if I sniffed hard enough a sweaty smell wafted up from inside the zip of my jacket. It wasn't just the outside temperature that was making me sweat. It was the nauseating anticipation of Ronan being there. Or not being there. Either way I felt panicky. Dad drove out through town onto the pier road. There was no one about as it was only six. The boats in the harbour were tinted bronze in the early morning sun.

*Saoirse* was tucked in between two small trawlers. All three boats were protected from the wind by the curved harbour wall. I strained my eyes but couldn't see any movement on board. There was no sign of Sean and my anxiety increased. What if the trip was off?

Dad pulled up alongside the mooring and switched his headlights off. We got out of the car and a gust of wind grabbed my hair, whipping it against my face. I pulled my hood up and stood feeling dejected while Dad got his bag from the boot.

Donal, in yellow oilskins, appeared on *Saoirse*'s deck and waved at us.

'Let's go lads,' was all he said, and we hurried to comply.

Dad un-moored the boat while I carried our bags on. I caught the ropes and coiled them carefully, not sure whether I was being watched. For all I knew, Ronan was standing in the wheelhouse grinning sarcastically at my fumbling efforts. Looking as aloof as possible I opened the door and walked into the welcome warmth of the little cabin.

'Ah. Just in time, we've tea.' Sean cleared a space on the bench and I sat down before he pressed a mug into my hand. He was alone.

'The wind's quieter now, so we should have a good trip,' he reassured me. 'Not that the rain's showing signs of stopping any time soon.' The cloud cover did seem very low and the island was invisible. I was just about to ask him about Ronan's whereabouts when Donal and my dad walked in.

'Let us get this show on the road,' said Donal. He knocked the engine into reverse and carefully manoeuvred *Saoirse* away from the trawlers.

As we turned out of the harbour into the Atlantic, the boat began to pitch and roll. Donal commented that it would get worse once we were away from the shelter of the cliffs, which wasn't what I needed to hear. My dad had certainly taught me a love of sailing, but he couldn't prevent my tendency to feel sick in rough seas. I prayed that it would soon pass and stared through the window towards the horizon, which seemed to help a bit and took my mind off it.

The trip passed quickly enough. I stayed inside, clutching my tea mug and ignoring the men's idiotic banter. I felt terribly let down that Ronan wasn't there. He must have known that I'd be on board and deliberately not come. Maybe my nausea was his fault, not the sea. My musings were interrupted by the backward thrust of the engine as Donal came alongside the island pier.

'I'm going off to help Donal,' Dad said. 'I haven't been out along the coast for a good long while. We'll be back to pick you two up later.'

I hadn't heard that decision being made but was happy enough to spend the time alone with Sean. I'd ask him about Trigve and no doubt be regaled with hilarious anecdotes. I needed a laugh and not having Dad's glum face around was a blessing really. We stood in the drizzle watching the boat pull away and then turned to walk up the path from the beach.

An assortment of waterproof birds stabbed invisible food along the shoreline. The tide was coming in fast and would soon be licking the bank of shingle at the very top of the beach. I realised that I hadn't seen the moon for ages and wondered if it was full; it looked like a high spring tide. The full moon in spring brings the highest and lowest tides of the year and, according to my dad, should also coincide with the spawning of some fish species. A big white bird with black wingtips flew over us as though to confirm my thoughts.

'Gannet!' Sean shouted, pointing upwards, his mouth open in a big grin.

At the same moment I saw it, I realised that I could smell the scent of turf burning in a fire. There was smoke billowing from the chimney of the derelict cottage. The broken door was still hanging on one hinge and the windows gaped, unglazed, so what was going on? A crunching on the shingle behind us made me turn around.

He was completely obscured with bright yellow waterproofs but there was no mistaking the loping walk. A roll-up sent a trickle of blue smoke from his right hand.

Ronan nodded as though he'd seen us the day before.

I peered through the drizzling rain, hoping for a little sign of intimacy from him.

'Come up, there's tea.' He pressed on in front of us and pushed open the creaky door. The fire smouldering in the grate wasn't the only homely touch. Rain dripped through the roof and slanted gently in through the windows. All the rubbish had gone and in a corner furthest from the door he'd rigged up a tarpaulin. It was big enough for sleeping under and protected his stuff from the rain. A makeshift table with some rickety chairs made a cheery scene. There were oil lamps, crockery and tea things on the table.

'But how come ... how long have you been here?'

He ignored me and hung a kettle over the embers.

'Will you eat?' he asked. An image of Tom in Maggie's kitchen came unbidden to mind. Tom could make tea and talk in long sentences with jokes thrown in, all at the same time. What was Ronan, this dour and awkward man, doing inside my heart?

# 23: ISLAND PEOPLE

After drinking tea the three of us made our way up the path towards the gannet rocks. Sean pressed on ahead, leaving me to walk with Ronan.

'My mother's family came from this island.' He spoke without looking at me.

'Really? When? Why did they leave?' My clumsy questions sounded idiotic as I asked them but I didn't care. At last he might tell me something about himself.

'They were one of the last families to go. That was my grandmother's cottage you just had your tea in. It was in the seventies they left.'

I heard his sorrow for the dispossessed family. 'Did you come here to visit when you were little?'

Ronan stopped walking and turned to me as he answered. 'No I didn't, not at all. I came here for the first time when my father brought me three years ago. He told me that my mother's family could never bring themselves to revisit the past. It was all too sad for them. After my mother died nobody would even mention the island. It was only when the last of the old people died that my father felt he could show me the house. He didn't have the same feeling for it. He met my mother when he was out here fishing with his father. She left the island with him, not thinking she might never come back here.'

Remembering the intimacy we'd shared in the tower I took a chance and reached for his hand. 'And you, are you planning to come back?' I asked, wondering what that would mean for me.

His hand responded to mine. We carried on walking, holding hands.

Ronan answered quietly. 'I love being here, Clare. I camp out in the old house when I can. It's only me now. Some of the old families used to come over to fish once in a while. You'll have seen the currach below? Everyone's gone now, dead or lost in a city somewhere. Nobody wants this kind of life anymore.'

'What about that dog?' I recalled the skinny, yellow-eyed dog.

'Oh, there are feral dogs here, descendants from our family's days. I'm supposed to be catching them. They are a threat to the ground nesting birds, the puffins and plovers. Sean's said he's organising a grant that will pay me for helping the project.'

So Sean had been talking to him. So much for my being part of Team Gannet!

We walked along in silence. I'd always been fascinated about the lives of island people up and down the coast of Ireland. My dad had told me how they rowed by currach to the mainland for provisions. Otherwise they lived hard but peaceful lives on the storm-swept islands. A lot of writers and poets came from the islands. As though sitting on a rock, surrounded by the wind and the sea, bred poetry into the people's souls. When we went to the Blasket Islands in County Kerry my mum had started crying. She'd said she didn't know why she was crying and wondered if it was just sorrow for the human condition.

Ireland is full of derelict beauty. Famine caused the abandonment of homesteads and the emigration of thousands upon thousands. The landscape is littered with ruins of castles, churches, houses and whole villages. The nature of stone cottages means that they tend to stay upright for centuries, their innards displayed for all to see.

I felt some excitement to be walking with an island man. Ronan was a true descendant of an ancient line of subsistence dwellers. His dark eyes took on new meaning for me as I remembered the stories about island folk and the seal people. Maybe he was, after all, descended from a line of selkies.

Of course I didn't really believe that, but a little part of me was attached to the notion of Ronan turning back into a seal when nobody was looking.

Sean had reached the west-facing cliff tops where he looked back at us with a big grin on his face.

'Come and see,' he mouthed. We couldn't hear him. The sea roared below us, and the wind had picked up as we'd climbed to higher ground. We struggled up the last ascent and stood panting at the top. The sea stacks were being pounded by huge bursting waves and looked smaller than usual. The high tide covered a lot of the smaller rocks too and had completely concealed the stony beach under the cliffs. Loud booms shook the ground each time a wave crashed through the caves beneath our feet. The place was alive with seabirds, oblivious to the weather. There were gulls and kittiwakes, guillemots and razorbills, shearwaters and fulmars, and there were gannets.

The gannets were huge in comparison with the other birds. There was a collection of mottled juveniles as well as mature birds. The whiteness of the adults' feathers seemed whiter than the gulls' and their yellow heads and black wing tips made them even more distinctive.

'I think we've fifteen pairs here.' Sean's eyes shone with excitement. 'Will you make the notes, Clare?' He picked up his binoculars. After a long pause during which he scanned each and every corner of the stacks he triumphantly turned to us.

'Make that twenty-three. We've twenty-three pairs and we have twenty-three nests, each with a single egg.' He hugged me and beamed at Ronan. 'Isn't it great? You have a gannet colony on your island. Now we wait and see how many hatch.' He pointed to a group of juveniles. 'And you see those youngsters over there? Passing birds will see them and may join the roost unless they're visiting from a site elsewhere. The fishing's so good here, I think there'll be a few more as summer comes on, not breeding but maybe planning for next year.'

He pulled a journal from his pocket and sat scribbling away with a look of pure joy on his boyish face.

I made my own notes, complete with doodle-like drawings, about the nests, peering at the scruffy bundles of twigs and seaweed to try and spot an egg. Most of the nests had one parent sitting, thus obscuring them. Some nests had both parents home. No egg had been left unattended.

I looked around, trying to count the juveniles, too. Several stood on ledges and there were immature as well as mature birds fishing near the cliffs. We watched one gannet soaring elegantly, thirty feet above the surging water. Suddenly it folded its wings and entered the water like a turbocharged paper plane. The transformation was dramatic, from lofty serenity to ballistic missile in half a second. All around us, birds were firing into the sea and coming up with fish in their beaks.

'They're fishing for mackerel,' Ronan said to no one in particular.

'No, it must be herring,' Sean countered. Ronan didn't answer but stared silently at the scene below. He told me later that he'd been fishing there all week and knew that the sea around them was alive with sprats and that the mackerel were beginning to arrive.

'Hey! Yes!' Sean shouted, pointing frantically and pulling at my coat. He began raising his binoculars but then lowered them. He didn't need them. First one, then another, then a group of at least a dozen fins broke the water's surface.

'Dolphins!' I shrieked. They were moving fast and when they got closer we could see their heads as they surfaced to breathe. The dolphins reached the fish, breaking up to form a circle around them. We were watching an organised fish-kill. Some of them slapped the surface with their tails to stun and confuse the fish. They leapt and twisted and sometimes left the water completely, flying in a graceful arc before landing with a tremendous splash.

All the while, gannets flashed past them, sometimes entering the sea dangerously close to the big grey mammals. Sean told us that very rarely a gannet had been known to hit a dolphin and break its neck. Gannets, he said, fly over the ocean watching for dolphins, as the dolphins can always find fish with their sonar. And sometimes the dolphins put their heads out of the water to look for gannets. If a human wanted to find fish, spotting groups of seabirds and dolphins together was always a good sign.

We huddled against the wind for another half an hour until the birds and dolphins had finished all the herring, or mackerel, or sprats, or whatever they'd been eating. The dolphins headed south and most of the gannets sat preening on the rocks. Some followed the dolphins south. Soon they were specks and then they disappeared completely.

Sean stood up and rubbed his hands.

'We were right; it's all been worth it. I just wish Liam had been here to see it. These gannets have been checking out this site for five years or more. They'll have been up here for the fishing and seen what great potential it has.'

He spoke to me like a teacher, staring and nodding encouragingly to get his message across. Ronan didn't seem to be listening.

'Where have they all suddenly come from?' I asked.

'They could have come down from Scotland, but we think they've probably come up here from the south, almost certainly from the Skellig Islands down in county Kerry,' he said. 'A breeding gannet will stay faithful to its nest, year after year. But a first-time breeder may choose to go elsewhere.'

'But I thought gannets went back to where they were born?' I asked through chattering teeth. I'd grown cold in the strong wind.

'Ah yes, that's often true, and we're not sure, but we think it has to be one of two things. First, their birth colonies may be crowded and these are first-time breeders who just couldn't get a foothold. They'll have been living away from home for two or three years, travelling down around the West African coast during the winter and as far north as Norway and Iceland in summer. They can fly hundreds of miles in a day, no bother.

'They'll have been flying over these stacks hundreds if not thousands of times in the last year or two. On the other hand, it could be there's better fishing up here. There is no doubt the seas are warming and just a few hundred miles further north can make a more favourable place for the fish to breed. Cold water plankton is what the fish need. The fishing has certainly been better between here and Donegal these last two years. They may have chosen not to go home to Kerry to breed because they know there won't be enough food there.'

Ronan nodded in agreement about the fishing and looked thoughtfully out to sea.

Sean picked up his binoculars and searched the ocean. There were white caps on the waves for as far as we could see.

'The weather's looking a bit dodgy,' he said.

'There's a storm coming in from out west,' Ronan answered. 'We should go down to the house. Saoirse's probably headed to Carran to drop the lobsters off, before it breaks. They'll not be back here now till after the tide's turned.'

I was elated to have been given more time with Ronan, with only Sean to worry about. We scrambled down the steep hill, slipping where rain had turned the path to mud. The cottage came into view with smoke blowing sideways from the chimney. The wind was evidently as strong down at sea level, and we reached shelter only seconds before the clouds burst open and drenched the shingle shore.

# 24: SEAL

Though the rain had eased, gale force winds rattled the cottage roof. The door banged repeatedly and cold air poured in through the empty window frames. Ronan's tarp was billowing but holding fast in the sheltered corner.

'I'm not sure how long you could live here in this weather,' Sean said.

Ronan smiled and carried on stoking the fire to make tea. He surprised us by setting a griddle pan to warm. Then he rummaged in his storage boxes and came up with ingredients for pancakes. I watched with my mouth watering as the batter bubbled and set, and Ronan plopped the small hot cakes onto a plate for us. My love for him grew. I'd no idea he could cook.

'There's some jam there, in that basket under the table, Clare,' he said while starting a second batch. He caught my eye, as he turned round to point at it. My spine fizzed with a pang of longing and I found myself audibly sighing.

Every ten minutes or so, one of us got up to spy through cracks in the door to look at the storm. There was no sign of *Saoirse*. An hour passed.

'Do you think they're ok?' I asked. A sudden thought of my poor dad staring at the sea with rain trickling through his thin hair made me worry for him.

'They'll wait in Carran,' Ronan said. 'And come later, when the storm's passed over.'

His confidence made me forget my fears of shipwrecks and drowning.

'They're probably in the pub,' said Sean. He stood up and stretched. 'I think I'll go back and check those birds again.' He got up and flashed me a look that I couldn't interpret. I wasn't sure whether to follow him or stay behind.

Ronan intervened. 'There were seals this morning on the black beach. I wondered if you'd like to see them.' I jumped up and pulled my coat on.

'I think she wants to see the seals,' said Sean, smiling at me. 'Come to think of it, I'll leave the birds in peace. I'll wait here in case the boat comes back, I wouldn't mind a bit of shut-eye.' Ronan threw him a blanket and went out through the door with me following like a puppy.

The rain had eased to a soft drizzle and bright silvered patches shone promisingly through the cloud cover. We took an old track that had been walked for centuries by the islanders. It hugged the coast with a gradual incline up to a headland. On a good day there might be a view of the mainland with its little ports and beaches but today we could hardly see our own hands. Patches of sea mist swirled in, bringing spray from the waves that stung our faces with salt. Ronan appeared oblivious to the weather but I tugged my coat close around me and pulled the drawstrings of my hood as tightly as they would go.

'The black beach is down there.' Ronan pointed into the fog to the outline of a bay nestled in between cliffs on one side and huge sloping slabs on the other. It looked as though a giant had picked up the land and then twisted it in a fit of rage.

We climbed down a narrow gulley and jumped the last three feet onto the beach. I gasped in surprise: what I'd taken for black sand was in fact solid rock. It was as though the beach was a fossil of itself.

The stone sloped gently down towards the shoreline and received waves from the now ebbing tide just as a sandy beach would.

'Over there, the seals were over there, under the cliffs.' Ronan led me across the slippery rock.

'The tide's going out now,' I muttered.

'And it won't be back until well after midnight,' Ronan grinned down at me.

'Oh, look, there's one.' I broke away and waited for him to follow. A seal lay by itself out in the centre of the slabs.

'Umm, Clare, I don't think you want to go near that one.'

It was too late, I'd already seen. The seal was dead. I walked towards it and crouched down. For some reason, the sight of it made me cry. I was embarrassed and tried to control myself, but couldn't. He stood and watched me juddering and sniffing, then tried to pull me up. I shook him off and stayed crouching and stroking the thick pelt.

'It's a female, isn't it?' I asked. Though its eyes were staring and its mouth was parted in a snarl, it had a fine pretty head.

'It reminds me of my mum.' I gulped and choked as more sobs came up from the depths. 'She's gone. She never came back that day after the party.' I looked pleadingly up at him as though he held the answers.

Apparently he had given it some thought and did have an answer.

'I wonder if your mother's a person in the wrong place,' he told me. 'She maybe has to go back to her people, her city.' Ronan was emphatic about it. 'Don't you think that we all have a voice calling us back to the wild? For me, it's a calling home to the island. Perhaps your mother's unhappy here by the sea. Her wild call is from the city, from people rather than nature. She's not meant to be tucked away caring for a family with a man who's obsessed with fish. She's maybe got other important things to do.'

'How come you know so much about my mother?' I protested.

'My dad seems to know her well. Says she has a nose for injustice, that she feels very strongly about politics and such things. He says she writes, that she's a journalist.'

'But I thought we were enough for her. God, I sound pathetic.' I stared down at the seal, trying not to cry. 'What happened to your mother? What was her name anyway?' I said. I was annoyed that he was so sure of himself. Something inside me wanted to hurt him.

He looked me straight in the eye and I saw a flash of anger. Then he looked down and spoke, 'My mother's name was Eimear. She was a bit like your mother but in a different way, another person in the wrong place. She couldn't settle on the mainland. She spoke only Irish, refused to accept English as a language. She never once came back here, but something strong was pulling her towards the island.'

Then he went quiet and stared out to sea. I looked up waiting for more. When it came he said it in a voice so small that I nearly asked him to repeat himself.

'She went off the boat, on a stormy day like this. My father never saw her go, just noticed that she wasn't there anymore.'

He turned to look at me and his voice grew normal again. 'The coast-guard and the helicopter came, her body was never found. It broke him for a while and that's why he never talks about her. I was seven. At least you're grown up. And your mother's not dead, Clare.' He didn't seem angry, was just stating facts.

I was ashamed but still hurt from his abandonment of me after the party. I was past caring and blurted it out. 'Why didn't you see me again?' I carried on looking at the seal, distracted by its intricate clawed flippers. I could imagine how they had evolved from land mammals' feet and tried to imagine them in shoes. I didn't look at Ronan.

He pulled me up and then started walking.

'Come on. That seal smells bad, let's get into some shelter out of the wind.'

He walked me over to a cave under the cliffs where the wind couldn't reach us. From our hideout he pointed out a group of seals that must have recently come ashore. They were all grooming themselves. I hadn't noticed them at all; they were so well camouflaged by the black rock. The wind and rain didn't seem a problem to them.

I pulled my hood back and tried to rearrange the hair that was stuck to my face, obscuring my vision. He reached out and pulled my hands away. Then he pushed the hair out of my mouth and eyes and bent his head towards me. First he nuzzled my neck. Then he licked my mouth.

'My salty darling. Is it the sea air or your tears that make you so salty?' Gently and very slowly he brushed his lips against mine.

When my mouth began to open he pressed harder and then we were kissing. By the time we parted I was dizzy and couldn't stop grinning. His eyes met mine. His tongue, his lips, his body pressed firmly against me, completed my desire. This dark man, this island man, had won me completely. This was the wild soul I'd met in my dreams.

# 25: SAOIRSE RETURNS

As Ronan and I discovered each other, things began to change. The seals, one by one, slid back into the sea. The tide receded further and the wind dropped. Rain turned to a fine mist and then stopped altogether. When I looked out of the cave mouth I could see the glimmer of a mainland beach. It was the long golden curve of Doughmore strand, the beach where the Norwegians had gone midnight surfing.

'We'd better get going. Sean will be sending out a search party.' Ronan grinned down at me.

I licked my swollen lips and gently touched my chin where Ronan's bristles had rubbed me raw. He took my hand and led me back to the gulley.

'Wait. I want to say goodbye.' I pulled him over to where the dead seal lay and stood looking at its salty head.

'I think you should go to visit your mother,' Ronan said. 'See her in her own place.'

'Mum does keep phoning to invite me to Dublin but I think she should come here to see me, and Dad.'

'Go and see her,' he repeated.

'Come on, let's go,' I said. 'My dad might be back. And your dad.' I laughed. It was funny to think what our dads would have said if they'd seen us in the cave.

From the top of the gulley the seal looked like one of the dark rocks that littered the beach. Up on the cliff we could see that the cloud to the west had dissolved, allowing streaks of blue to show through.

'Hey, the sun's seen us and come to say hello.' Ronan opened his arms to the sky and shouted: 'We're here!'

The sun didn't pour down on us so Ronan obviously wasn't a sun god but I felt as though he had lightened. And everything had lightened for me. He took my hand and looked into my eyes.

'I've never met anyone like you.'

'Me, too,' I answered, burying my head in his chest with embarrassment.

'It's in our souls, Clare. I can feel it.'

So he felt it, too. If he was the wild soul of my dreams, perhaps I was the wild soul of his.

When we arrived at the cottage he pulled me away from the doorway and kissed me again. We moved back from each other when we heard Sean stirring inside.

'Come on,' he said. 'Let's go down and stand on the headland. *Saoirse* should be on her way.'

I stumbled after him, dazed and wobbly on my feet like something just born. I was an imprinted duckling, blindly following him out through the door. Everything about him was perfect. That dark hair, skimming the collar of his jacket and his worn jeans and scuffed boots were the coolest clothes I'd ever seen. The way he looked at me, half smile, half frown; it turned me to jelly. Nothing else mattered and I prayed that the boat would not return.

'Ah, look,' he said. 'That's her now.' The sun had lit up the sea and the big waves of earlier on had all but vanished. A shining dot began to grow until there was no doubt that it was a boat. As the sea took on green hues the shiny dot became the familiar blue hull of *Saoirse*.

'Will you come back with us?' I asked.

'No, I'm staying for a while. I've things to do here and it's the best thing.' He looked away as he spoke.

I felt my stomach drop with disappointment.

'But, ok, so when will I see you?' I asked, trying to sound casual.

'You're involved with the project, right?' He paused and smiled at my crestfallen expression. 'Don't be so sad and come back soon.'

That was all I needed. My spirits soared again and I didn't mind that as the boat approached he turned back into another person, separating his hand from mine and walking in front of me while I staggered and tripped along the shingle beach.

# 26: DOLPHINS

On the journey back to Carran, Dad invited Sean to move into the tower.

'It's not as if we haven't the room. You can have my old study; all my gear is up in the tower now. To be truthful, it would be great for us. Things can get a bit quiet what with Orla away so much.'

Sean looked delighted.

'And,' added Dad, 'I was thinking of inviting the Norwegian lads along, too, when they come back. They can sleep in the room under the observatory.'

At this Sean's face broke into an uncontrollable grin.

It was brilliant news: a house full would cheer Dad up, and would be a welcome distraction from my obsessive thoughts about Ronan.

'That'd be great, when do we start?'

Dad stroked his chin. 'I was thinking I'll ask Maggie to make up a room for you this week some time.'

'I can do it today,' I piped up. I loved the idea of having Sean around. Apart from anything else, I could make sure that he always took me to the island with him.

'Ok so, good idea, we'll go and collect your stuff on the way back so.'

Despite the good news about Sean I was in turmoil. I couldn't imagine when I'd have a chance to see Ronan again. And besides, he was so ethereal. He could ignore me the next time we met as though nothing had happened. I left the wheelhouse and stared back towards the island. Lit by the evening sun, it stood out like an emerald in the silvery sea. The house and its occupant had disappeared. The dream was over. A hand on my shoulder made me jump.

'Oh Sean, you scared me,' I smiled weakly at him.

'You look sad,' he said. 'Tell me about him,' he added with a wink.

'What do you think he's doing, staying there on his own?' I asked. 'What does Donal think about it?' I knew Sean wouldn't have the answers but he was easy to talk to and he had obviously spoken to Ronan about the island.

'Come on inside. There's a flask of hot tea in here.' He led me back into the warm cabin and began quizzing Donal.

'So, Donal, what is that son of yours doing on the island?' Sean gave me a conspiratorial glance as he spoke.

Donal didn't speak for a full minute. Then he turned round and addressed his answer to me.

'Ronan is very like his mother,' he stated. 'Ever since he was a small boy he's been a restless soul. When he was old enough to understand where his mother came from, he pestered me to take him to the island. I couldn't do that while Eimear's mother was alive. She wouldn't even have the island mentioned in her company. Leaving Carrig na Ron broke her heart. Now that she's dead and Ronan has seen the old house, I don't think he'll sleep easy on the mainland again. I'm telling you, Clare; he'll not rest away from that island.'

I felt Dad watching me. He scratched his head, making his hair look crazy, and peered at us. The fact he'd not brought his glasses would explain the peering, but it occurred to me that he'd have no idea why Donal was addressing his comments to me. To Dad, Ronan was just one of the crowd of young folk. If he sussed out what Donal meant, he'd be giving me a lecture later about how it would only mean heartache for me. He'd told me before how the island people had a troubled history. And how they were dark, deep people who, since leaving their home, tended to spend too much time staring at the sea or else leaving and never coming back. Even I could see that Ronan had not inherited his father's droll nature. He was quiet and thoughtful much like, I supposed, his mother.

I saw, too, that Donal knew I'd been bewitched by his island boy. What a crowd we were. He'd had his heart captured by an island woman and my dad had fallen for a city girl. I blushed and looked away, busying myself with tidying the cups and hoping somebody would change the subject.

'Hey look! Visitors!' shouted Sean, who'd wandered out of the wheelhouse. A familiar splash at the front of the boat had me running outside. I grabbed the anchor cable for support and hung my head over the side of the starboard bow.

A group of five dolphins were riding the bow wave, twisting and turning to keep up with the movement and every now and again one would sheer off and leap out of the water to take a breath. I let my hand trail down in the hope that one might reach up to touch me. Occasionally the one nearest did swivel its head and look up. I liked to think that they enjoyed watching me as much as I did them.

I wished Ronan could have been with me to see them. Then I realised I could feel his presence in the dolphins, as though he'd sent them to me with a message. I clearly understood that the dolphins were telling me to live in the moment. Life goes on, death goes on. Meetings and partings, they're all part of the cycle. Nothing is certain. Everything passes as surely as the bow wave was passing. As each dolphin took a breath and each wave broke, a moment had gone, never to return. I lay on the bow until long after the dolphins disappeared, staring down into the green water, missing him and very much missing my mother.

# 27: THE MOON AND THE TIDES

Three long weeks later May arrived with early summer warmth. I sat in the tower with Dad while he made little entries into his notebook from a pile of scruffy looking papers. As he finished with each paper, he triumphantly screwed it into a ball and we took turns throwing them at the waste-paper basket. I'd managed to get all but one of mine into the bin. His had mostly bounced off the wall onto the floor, which explained why the tower was usually in such a mess.

As he worked we reminisced about times past when we'd celebrated the old Celtic festival of Beltane on May eve. He used to make a big bonfire down by the yew hedge and we'd all sit next to it planning the summer ahead, with Mum and Dad drinking toasts to their good fortune.

I remember helping light the Beltane fire. Mum once made me dance around it with her, saying it would bring us good luck, make the vegetables grow and the fruit set. I thought about the year before when Dad told us that it was just a relief to know winter was over and the fish would be spawning. Mum had sighed and raised her eyes to the sky.

This summer was a bleak prospect without her. I hated my granny for a moment and felt sure that Mum could have come home more often if she'd really wanted to. There was definitely something bad happening between Mum and Dad. She sounded normal enough on the phone though, so maybe I was only imagining things. But I knew I wasn't.

Sean shouted up from the bottom of the stairs. 'I'm away to Carran. Will you come and check the emails with me?'

Dad didn't need persuading and snapped his notebook shut. I asked if I could come. He began interrogating me about my revision but then softened. I had been home alone a lot lately and was evidently working hard.

I think we'd both been in mourning, neither daring to ask the other about what was going on.

I'd no idea whether Mum and Dad were speaking and I'd no intention of confiding in him about Ronan and how I hadn't heard a thing from him since that day on the island. Sean had been out there with Donal while I'd been in exams or revision classes. He said Ronan was busy fishing with his dad and seemed cheerful enough.

'Come on, love,' Dad said with welcome warmth in his smile. 'I'll buy us all lunch at The Atlantic.' He went ahead of me to change into his good jacket.

Sean and Dad went to the internet café. Sean was applying for more research funding and Dad was chasing the university for money as well. His funding was always precarious so he marked exam scripts and supervised postgraduate students to make a bit more. Sometimes he went off to give papers and for teaching days, but he hadn't been anywhere for ages.

I left them to it, and having at least an hour to kill before lunch, found myself drawn, as I often did, to the pier. There was no sign of *Saoirse*, so I supposed she must be out fishing. I sat on a bollard watching the sea. The day was warm and little sparkles tipped the lapping water.

A cormorant sat on the roof of a rusty old trawler moored at the end of the pier. It held its wings out to dry and I wondered where it lived and whether it had a nest or a partner. A voice behind me made me jump. It was Bridie Healey, who asked about my dad. She was waiting for Donal to come back from the sea with lobsters and for another boat that was due to arrive with fish. She told me it was a great year for mackerel. They'd begun to arrive in large shoals from pelagic waters way out in the Atlantic.

'You can tell your father and Sean there'll be no shortage of food for their gannets this year. The herring are scarce enough now, but what does a gannet care when it can fill up with mackerel? Here, give me a hand, would you,' she said. I walked with Bridie to the little car park at the harbour wall, and helped her to set up a trestle table.

'We should make a bit of money today,' she said as she pulled out a battered red tin and placed it with a firm clunk onto the table. 'Here, sit with me a while, I have tea.' She poured two cups of sweet milky tea and sighed with relish as the hot liquid hit her throat.

'Ah, that's better. I've not sat down all day. Now, tell me how you are.'
She gave me a knowing look. 'I saw you gazing out to sea, are you hoping
for a certain young man to appear?' I saw that denial would be useless under
Bridie's fierce blue gaze. Her eyes were as piercing as a gannet's. I didn't
speak but nodded in agreement and shrugged.

Bridie carried on: 'He's worth waiting for, that young man. He'll be a
good husband to somebody some day. But not for you,' she added with a
frown. 'Sure you'll be wanting to go off to college and travel the world. You
wouldn't want to live here counting lobsters all your life. That boy doesn't
need any more heartache.'

I was upset that she could think me capable of hurting Ronan. I could
think of nothing better than counting lobsters all day as long as he was with
me.

'I suppose,' I said. I really didn't want to discuss it with anybody, least of
all Bridie. She had known Ronan since his childhood and was probably the
nearest thing he had to a mother. I changed the subject to fish.

'Are mackerel supposed to spawn at the full moon like the herring?'

Bridie looked at the water for a while and then she answered: 'I think the
moon affects us all. I had my babies at the full moon and I know others who
did too. Why wouldn't fish, which feel the pull of the tides, be the same?
What I don't understand is why anybody would spend his days studying
that.'

She was obviously referring to Dad's work.

'Do you not think there's more your father could do, Clare? Sure he used
to go off travelling all the time. What's happened to him lately?'

I had never considered that his work could be bad for him. All those
years, spying on the moon and the tides. Maybe Bridie was right. Maybe he
needed a fresh start.

'I'd better go,' I said. 'Dad and Sean are meeting me at The Atlantic.'

Bridie squeezed my hand and told me to tell Dad that the chowder
would be especially good at the pub today.

'Call down with Liam before you go home, won't you.'

I walked away thinking about what Bridie had said. I hoped that when I
came back after lunch *Saoirse* would be in with news of Ronan.

# 28: MACKEREL AND HERRING

After following Bridie's advice and lunching on the pub's famous chowder that was packed with fish and mussels, we wandered along the seafront towards the pier. Sunshine had turned the little town from a drab grey harbour to a bright seaside port. It wasn't quite ice-cream weather but the three of us had left our coats in the car. We turned our faces to the sky, hungry for light after what seemed like endless dark weeks of rain.

'I think May's my favourite month.' Dad said this every year. 'The blackbirds are singing and eggs are laid. And we have the whole summer ahead of us.' He smiled at us for a moment, before his face dropped and he stared at the ground deep in thought.

I knew he was thinking about Mum and tried to think of something cheery to say. But then as we turned the corner by the harbour wall, I felt my stomach lurch. *Saoirse* was in, tied to the mooring bollards and bobbing in the wake of the trawler that was now leaving the harbour. *Sea Star*, a black fishing boat, had tied up behind her.

Bridie stood behind the stall and a few people milled about. Donal's car was parked, boot open, beside the makeshift shop. He appeared from behind it with the skipper of *Sea Star*. Together they lifted boxes of mackerel onto a stand next to the stall. The milling people immediately formed a queue. More boxes appeared and then Donal drove the fifty yards back down to his own boat.

'Come on,' Dad said. 'He'll be in a rush now to get the lobsters away. We'll give him a hand.'

We walked past Bridie and her customers, giving her a wave as we did so. Her silver fish gleamed like treasure and I thought about how they would have been swimming around in the morning sun. They'd be in someone's frying pan before nightfall. *Sea Star*'s skipper stood behind Bridie. He swiftly picked fish from the box, gutted them, rinsed them in a barrel of seawater and slapped them down beside her.

A line of herring gulls stood in attendance on the harbour wall, crooning and yipping as they waited for the humans to leave them to the pile of discarded fish guts.

*Saoirse*'s decks were stacked with boxes of lobsters. The men formed a chain. Sean and Dad waited on board and Donal packed them into the back of the Range rover. I tried to help Donal but just got in the way; he was skilled and efficient on his own. He shouted at me to go and pick up some lobster pots from the foredeck that had been brought in for repair.

I propped them next to others on the quay, then waited while they loaded the lobsters. Someone had already tied their claws with elastic bands but the hapless creatures still clacked uselessly around on top of each other. I tried not to look.

The men talked as they worked. Donal decided it was a grand day for a visit to the island. He knew the marine institute would pay him and he was free all afternoon.

'We'll make a day of it. Bridie's been asking for a while, she might like to come. We'll all go.'

I hadn't been to the island since the nest count. This was partly because of the weather, partly because of school, and partly because Sean had a feeling that the gannets wouldn't brood their eggs so happily if they were disturbed. It was a crucial time for the fragile colony. I'd been so patient that suddenly I couldn't bear it any more. I had to see him. As if in answer to my prayers Donal turned to me.

'Ronan was asking after you. Will you come with us today?'

I couldn't believe it. Ronan had asked about me. He wanted to see me. I tried to look calm.

'Yeah, sure, whatever,' I said, trying not to grin my head off.

Donal drove away with Dad, shouting: 'Ten minutes.'

They'd gone to unload his catch into a refrigerated lorry that would be waiting to take the lobsters off for export. The precious crustaceans would be flown from the nearest airport to the hotel kitchens of London, Paris and who knew where else. I sat with Sean on the bollards.

'Funny to think that those fellows were dancing around on the seabed and never knew they'd be in Paris one day,' said Sean.

'I can't bear to think about them, they must be terrified,' I replied.

'Oh, I'm not sure lobsters think about things that much,' he said. And then, as his life's work was dependent on the slowing of climate change, he started a little speech about air freighting food, luxury food at that. As I nodded glumly at him, he changed the subject and told me about his emails.

'We heard from the lads today. They're arriving at the weekend. Being air freighted themselves! And we heard from the Irish fisheries people. This is the best mackerel season we've had for years. Especially up along this more northerly part of the coast. Is it global warming? Who knows? Maybe all those storms have brought them in from the ocean waters, but whatever it is, the sea's alive with them.'

Sean grinned enthusiastically and I stopped thinking about lobsters clacking about in the dark hold of a plane somewhere.

'What about Dad's herring? Is there any more news of them?' I looked at him laughing at the thought of news from a shoal of fish.

'Liam and our Norwegian friends have lost the bet.' Sean's face became serious again. 'The herring haven't done so well. The mackerel have won hands down. The salmon's not great this year, either. And we heard from our Scottish gannet people. The sand eels just aren't there, fished out or moved towards Scandinavia, it seems. So thank God for the mackerel, our gannets will be happy.'

'So Ronan was right about that,' I interrupted, happy to be saying his name out loud.

I knew that mackerel were too big for the puffins and my favourite little black birds, the guillemots. But at least there were sprats in these waters. There were always plenty of them in the summer.

'Dad said the puffins in Scotland lost most of their young last year,' I told Sean.

'I know, love, with the sand eels gone, times are hard for our sea birds. The gannets may be the only good news this year so let's hope we get some chicks out on the island.'

We chatted about the habits of gannets and then walked up to see Bridie. She'd finished her brisk trade. There wasn't one fish left. I helped her collapse the trestle table and then the three of us sat in the sun watching the hungry gulls scoffing their reward, waiting for Donal and Dad to return.

# 29: STRAY DOGS

I spent the trip to the island worrying about whether I'd be able to get Ronan by himself, as far away from my dad and Dridie as possible. She had joined us with a cooler bag of supplies for him, so what with Dad, Donal and Sean, as well, it would be busy.

Also, Sean wanted me to come and help count the gannets and make records in the little book he'd given me. I hadn't got it with me and didn't dare confess this to Sean. Still, I could copy my notes out later. When he'd given me the book, he'd told me to keep it with me at all times for jotting down ideas and impressions as well as sightings. I wouldn't make a very good field researcher, I thought, leaning on the railings staring down at the sea.

The rails smelled of paint. They had been touched up since my last time on board. The smell of diesel and paint together was making me queasy. The water was like clear green glass, shot through with shafts of sunlight. It was a perfect day for spotting seals or dolphins and I spent the whole of the trip scanning the waves for the telltale sight of a round dark head or a thorn-shaped fin. There were no marine mammals to be seen but what I did notice were the gannets.

As *Saoirse* approached the island, the bright white birds were constantly soaring over. Looking through Sean's binoculars I could see them bend their necks to peer down at us with glinting eyes. Some of the birds had the dark spots of juvenile plumage but the majority were pure white with distinctive black wing tips and the classic yellow head of sexually mature gannets. Sean said that as well as the adults who were nesting on the stacks, there would be visitors from the south up for a few hours fishing.

Ronan stood on the quay waiting for the mooring lines. He had one hand in his pocket. The other held the smoking remnants of a roll up.

I hung back while he and Dad secured the boat. Then, helping Bridie with her bag, we managed to avoid eye contact for a further few minutes. Finally, as everybody was walking up the shingle, he stood behind me and breathed a mumbled greeting into my ear. I turned and looked straight into his eyes.

'Hello, green eyes,' he said.

Then, when we were momentarily out of sight, he grabbed me and kissed me with desperate passion. I was so grateful that I felt faint, but then annoyed. How could he always assume that I wouldn't reject him? It wasn't fair. I wouldn't have dared do the same to him. I let him take my hand anyway and together we followed the others.

Although I felt shy in front of the grown ups, I didn't want to let go of his hand. Dad seemed not to notice and Sean winked at me. Bridie avoided my eyes but gave Ronan a long look. Donal ignored us and asked Ronan if he could make them all some tea to go with the apple pie Bridie had brought along.

Having stoked the fire and showed his dad the tea things, Ronan took my hand again and led me away.

'We'll leave them for a while, I've something to show you.'

I followed him up some overgrown steps into a little thicket of thorn bushes. Though the way was dense and prickly, a path had been hewn that opened into a clearing. Hidden behind a group of stunted trees, and crawling with brambles, was a derelict barn. It was a sad sight. The roof had caved in and the walls were on their way down.

There was no door, though a makeshift collection of wood had been fashioned to make a half door. I thought about the busy life the barn would once have been home to. Perhaps Ronan's own family would have stored hay or kept winter herds in out of the rain.

Ronan opened the door and beckoned me over. I heard a low growling and saw that the little yellow-eyed bitch was inside. She looked even thinner than the last time and the reason why was plain to see. A grown puppy crouched behind her. The youngster was bigger than its mother but the bitch's teats were swollen enough to assume that it was still suckling from her.

'Where's the dad?' I asked.

'There's a skinny black sheepdog around that I haven't been able to catch,' answered Ronan. 'The pup has a collie look about him, don't you think?'

I agreed, and it would explain why it was so big compared to the whippet mum.

'Will you catch him, too?' I asked.

'Yes, I have to, and then that's all, I think. No one's seen any other dogs these last two years although there used to be more. I wonder if this bitch is part fox, she has such bright yellow eyes. I've not seen a fox around, though.'

'What are you going to do with them?' I asked.

Ronan gave me a big smile and said, 'I was hoping you could help me there. They'll be put to sleep otherwise. I can't keep them here so I was hoping you'd have some ideas.'

I felt a desperate need to help both him and the dogs but was sure that Dad would say no to taking on two extra dogs.

'Well, I'll try and think of something. I'll let you know.'

'I was hoping you'd take them today. It's for the sake of the project. We can't have dogs running about the place, especially this young male. And there's no doubt she's been hunting for him. The place was full of feathers when I found them.'

I said I'd talk to Dad and then I turned to him.

'Is that the only reason you wanted to see me?' I looked down as I said it in case the answer was yes. He didn't say anything but pulled something from his pocket.

'I made you this.'

He handed me a smooth wooden object.

'It's made from a piece of driftwood I had saved for a rainy day.'

He'd fashioned the wood into a tiny seal. The detail was extraordinary. Each whisker and claw had been carefully carved. The seal had the same sleek lines of the dead seal on the black beach, but somehow there was a shine to its eyes that made it seem alive. I touched my lips to it and then looked at him. He hugged me to him and began to kiss me. His chin was rough with stubble again but I didn't care and hungrily kissed him back. His hand was creeping up my jumper when a shout made us both jump.

We turned to see Sean landing on his knees with a loud 'Bollocks!' He looked up apologetically.

'Sorry folks, didn't mean to interrupt but we're going up to the site.'

He pulled himself away from the bramble that had tripped him and brushed himself down. I pulled my ruffled clothes together and followed the men back along the prickly path.

# 30: GANNET CHICKS

Ronan led the way up to the cliff-top viewpoint. It seemed he knew his way around the site better than Sean now. I ran to keep up with him while Dad and Sean brought up the rear. As we climbed, the vegetation changed from scrub to short grass dotted with sea pinks. A bumblebee droned from flower to flower, bumping off the gaudy tufts like a miniature drunken helicopter. The island glistened with sunlit spider's gossamer and early summer scents perfumed the bright day. The sea breathed a lazy rolling swell. It was rare to be walking up here without fighting the wind. Ronan rolled a cigarette and looked content as he climbed effortlessly to the top. I, on the other hand, was panting and sweating.

When we reached the peak, a fresh southwesterly breeze reminded me that the wind never left the cliffs and stacks. There weren't many birds in the air. The gannets and other cliff-nesters had finished their morning fishing spree and were having an afternoon rest. They slept, preened or fiddled with nesting material. Many of the nests had both parents at home. Very soon the place would be alive with squawking youngsters.

Movement caught my eye. A lone gannet, whose mate must have been away fishing, flapped its wings and stood up for a stretch. I thought I saw a dark bundle, the size of a pear, crouching in the nest. I nudged Dad and he passed me his binoculars.

Naked but for a thin white down, the black chick lay still, with its eyes closed. I prayed it was alive. There were traces of broken eggshell in the nest.

In answer to my prayers the chick's other parent fell from the sky and offered food to the hatchling, which greedily snatched it. The gannet settled on the chick and its mate began preening at the edge of the nest before taking off on a fishing expedition of its own.

Ronan pulled me to the other side of a hillock, away from the gannetry. I glanced back and saw Dad and Sean disappearing out of sight towards the stacks. We settled in the wind shadow of a little grassy bank. He stroked my face and kissed me again. Then he pulled away and looked worried.

'I hate to be up here disturbing them, you know,' he said, glancing back over his shoulder. 'Listen to them, you can hear them from here.' He was talking about Sean and dad. 'I like it best when there's nobody here. The birds and the seals don't want anyone watching them.'

And nor did he, I supposed. He lay back in the grass with his eyes shut. I wondered if that included me but didn't like to ask and contented myself with lying next to him, listening to the birds and the drone of Sean and Dad. Rolling onto his stomach Ronan crawled to the edge of the cliff. I did the same and we watched the sea far below us swirling in and out of a hollow it had made. I was dreamily following the back and forth movement of kelp. It looked like a witch's long green hair being washed and rinsed in the current. He turned onto his back and started talking about his dreams.

'It's strange,' he confided. 'Since coming here I feel happier than I've ever been. In my right place, I suppose. But I have nightmares. I don't know if it's the cottage or what. I wake up suffocating and I'm drowning in dark Water, but I'm not really awake, and it happens over and over again.'

'We both have the same dreams,' I mumbled. He didn't answer and I stroked his face. He was pale for a man who lived outside. For the first time I felt like the strong one. Leaning over I kissed him with quick little kisses, gently like you would a puppy or a baby. My hair fell over his face, he pulled it away and rolled me on to my back. I think if my dad hadn't been nearby we would have at last made love there on the windy hill. As it was he groaned and pulled me up to kneeling.

We kissed one more time, with me looking over his shoulder in case Dad could see. When we heard them approaching we hurriedly broke apart. Following them down the hill, Ronan and I held hands until the cottage came into view. Then he dropped away from me, seeming to disappear.

'I'll get the dogs,' he said, jogging towards the barn before I had time to go with him. I waited with Sean while Dad went aboard *Saoirse* to join Donal and Bridie in the wheelhouse, out of the wind.

After Ronan had handed the makeshift leads to us, he stood back from the quay watching us drag the reluctant dogs up a small ramp onto the stern deck. I was confused at the way he'd been so loving one minute and then practically ignoring me the next. I wondered if it was something to do with his dad and Bridie being there. But they were out of view now. Surely he could blow me a secret kiss or something.

As *Saoirse*'s engine throbbed into life I waved my goodbyes. He gave a brief nod and turned on his heel as though I was a passing acquaintance. If I hadn't been clutching the seal in my pocket, I think I would have given up on him there and then. But as it was, I felt the love and care that imbued the wood and accepted it as enough to sustain me until our next meeting.

# 31: NEW PUPPY

Tom closed the gate and stood for a moment watching the ewes and lambs. The flock lived outside now and was in good shape. Snowball, the pure black lamb, had grown as strong as the others. The horses grazed contentedly by the sheep as Tom leaned his back against the gatepost, his face turned to the sunshine. The sky twittered with skylarks as I ran across the field to join him.

'Hey Tom,' I kissed him on the cheek in a flurry of sweaty breathlessness. 'Oh, I'm glad I found you. Cait said you'd be here'.

He grinned, obviously pleased to see me.

'Please help me. Please say yes. I've something to show you.' Walking back towards the farmhouse I looked over my shoulder to check that he was following. He was, of course. As we walked he heard the barking.

'That's funny,' he said. 'That's not Spats' bark. Who's here?'

Cait stood by the barn door with her hand down the back of Joe's jeans. Joe had his arm around her and was nuzzling her hair. The barking was coming from inside the barn. We looked in and I watched Tom's face with concern as he took in the brown bitch and her black and white pup.

'I thought maybe you could train it and sell it or something. Please Tom, it'll be put to sleep otherwise,' I begged.

Tom, looking from the dogs to me and back again, said he wasn't sure he could cope with a puppy, what with college and everything. His mother would be bound to say no and Spats would have something to say about it, too. But Cait reminded him that he'd be home for the haymaking in June and then he'd have the whole summer. And it did look like a good dog.

'It does look a bit like old Spots, doesn't it?' he said to Cait. 'I suppose we could do with a good sheepdog now that he's gone. I can't take the bitch though, she'll have to go somewhere else.'

I hugged Tom. I'd known he wouldn't be able to say no. He was such a softy.

He checked the pup over and scratched its chest. Smiling, he turned to me and asked where the dogs had come from. When I told him about Ronan and the island he looked away, crestfallen. He must have seen then that this wasn't a gift from me to him but that I was doing it for Ronan.

I felt guilty and I also had a nagging worry about how Maggie would feel when she found out I'd brought the puppy from Ronan. She was funny with me about Ronan. Whenever he was mentioned, her voice became clipped and cold. I knew that she was a close friend of Bridie's and I could only imagine what they'd been saying to each other.

Also, she knew how Tom felt about me and I suppose she couldn't help disliking the fact that he mooned over me while I turned my heart elsewhere.

'I'll do it if you'll help,' he said firmly. I sensed his motive, of course, but thought it would be fun anyway. And the main thing was that the pup was saved.

'Agreed,' I said. 'Sheepdog training assistant at your service.' I gave him another hug.

'What about the bitch?' Cait asked.

'I dunno,' I said. 'I'll have to keep her till we sort something.'

Tom looked at the dogs thoughtfully. 'We'll separate them now. Cait, would you feed the pup and I'll run Clare home.'

'It's ok,' I interrupted. 'My dad's car's here, Sean's been teaching me to drive and Dad said it'd be ok to drive it just to here and back.' Leading the bitch away from her grown pup, I walked towards the car. I could feel Tom staring after me and felt sorry that my feelings for him were so platonic. He was a good man with a big heart to have taken on such a commitment. After a fifteen-point turn, I waved goodbye to them all and, crashing the gears, made my way up the hill towards the tower.

In my dream that night I was swimming to the island. I never seemed to get any closer. I woke gasping for air. Was this what drowning felt like? Lying in the dark, longing for my elusive dark-eyed man, I couldn't get back to sleep.

# 32: THE MARINE CENTRE

It was the day the Norwegians were due to come back. Maggie shut the fridge door as I staggered sleepily into the kitchen one Saturday morning in late May. It was nearly midday. I hadn't seen Ronan since the day with the dogs, eighteen long days, and was desperate to finish my exams and go back to the island.

Even though I spent a lot of time revising, I couldn't focus and the exams hadn't gone very well so far. I didn't dare tell Dad but none of the right questions had seemed to come up. I was very worried I might fail. All I could do was daydream about Ronan lying on his back with me kissing him and feeling him respond. Then I'd see his troubled eyes recalling his dark dreams.

I'd taken to doing my revision in the tower just so that I could look out at the island and imagine him looking back at me.

'There you are, Clare,' said Maggie. 'Tell Liam the fridge is stocked and there's a casserole on the side. Donal will be up later with lobster for the lads. And he'll bring the beer.' She swept a last look around the sparkling room and took her apron off.

It was great having Maggie around. The frostiness I'd felt from her when I first got together with Ronan seemed to have vanished since the exams started. In fact she'd been very supportive, knowing how much I was missing Mum. She drove Cait and I down to the school most days and always invited me in for tea on the way home. Tom was back at college and wouldn't be home till haymaking time. Our house felt so much cosier since Dad asked her to help. The window over the sink was open, allowing garden scents to mingle with the garlicky cooking smells. The dogs, including the little brown bitch, had been banished to the wood barn and our cheeky cats lay on a stolen patch of sunlight in Oscar's bed.

Still feeling very sleepy, I decided to make a proper coffee. The ritual always brought Mum to mind. If she'd been here she'd have frothed hot milk for us, and stood outside puffing away on a cigarette. Then she'd have walked round the garden exclaiming about the wondrous flowers and insects that miraculously reoccurred every year. She'd told me the night before that Granny had had to go back into hospital, but that her sister might come over again so that she'd be able to get down for a weekend. But I told her not to worry because I had a feeling she might try to block my relationship with Ronan.

I was so desperate to see him again that I didn't want anything stopping any possible chances to see him. Soon my exams would be over and I'd be able to go with Sean every day. I couldn't wait and couldn't stop dreaming about what would happen when we finally got to spend some time on our own.

I poured Dad a coffee and went up to the tower to see him, and to look over to the island, of course. He took his mug and we sat admiring the lovely day. Each window held a new joy. In the south, a stand of cherry trees resplendent in their candyfloss gowns, like a group of gossiping bridesmaids. Below us, the fresh green of young birch leaves and, from the west window, a quiet sea, perfectly blue and still as a watercolour. In the middle of it, the island, a basking dragon, stretched out snoring peacefully in the morning sun. And somewhere along its folded flanks was Ronan.

'Do you know, Clare,' Dad broke into my reverie. 'I've realised, I completely forgot to look out for the full moon.'

I looked at him with pretend shock at his revelation.

'I no longer know nor care about the spawning habits of herring,' he stated. My shock became real. I knew Dad didn't comb his hair much, and that we had to remind him to eat these days, but he did always seem to be working. At least he was always shuffling his papers about. I felt the ground beneath me sway ever so slightly as it occurred to me that maybe my dad was having a breakdown.

I didn't know what to say about the herring or the moon but luckily Sean appeared in the stairwell with a mug of coffee, having smelled it in the kitchen on his way over.

'Liam, Clare, grand day for it.' He eased his mug and himself onto a window ledge and looked at his watch. He was shaved, brushed and polished and kicking his heels back against the wall like a kid.

'Jesus, Sean, it won't make him arrive any sooner,' Dad said.

'No, no, it's not just that, I've had a brainwave, folks.' He went on, smiling. 'I've taken the liberty of emailing a few people and now I have a proposal for you.' He paused for attention and went on: 'You know, Liam, how you're always saying the tower's too empty and lonely without Orla. And you know how you're always worrying about the research funding drying up? What would you say, then, to us opening a marine centre here?'

Dad looked bemused. Then he smiled for the first time in weeks.

'Go on, tell me more,' he said, getting off his stool.

'Well, I reckon it's perfect. A little far from the sea perhaps, but only a five minute car ride. The hostel in Carran is a joke and there's nowhere safe there for us to leave our equipment. With the island becoming a nesting site for gannets, it will be declared a reserve and will need stewardship. What with the observatory and all the room you've got here, we could house everybody: marine biologists, ornithologists, the lot.'

Dad looked stunned and then beamed at him. 'Sean, that's brilliant. Do you really think we could? It would become the place I always had in mind. Do you think we could get any funding?'

'Just say the word, Liam, and I'm on to it. Look, we could even tie it in with an education thing for schools, maybe even do nature boat trips for tourists and the like. You just need to give it the thumbs up and we'll find the people to sort it.'

Dad walked over to Sean and shook his hand.

'This is the best thing I've heard since the day the builders finished the dome. Let's make some phone calls before the Norwegians arrive.'

Going back down to the kitchen, leaving them sorting a list of people to phone and email, I wondered what Ronan would say about tourists going anywhere near his precious island.

The dogs would be dry by now so I went to the barn to get them. Oscar and Mac leaped ahead but the brown bitch hung back.

'We'll have to give you a name, won't we?' She cocked her head as I spoke. Although my dad had said there was no way I could keep the little dog, her yellow eyes had got under my skin and his, too. I knew that I'd win him round and I decided then and there to call her Amber.

# 33: PRESENTS

The Norwegians came bearing gifts. The treasures of Norway were laid out on the kitchen table. There were a variety of goat's cheeses including a brown one that tasted like fudge. A collection of differently shaped jars contained herrings in various types of pickling juices.

'Roll mops. Lovely,' said Dad appreciatively.

'Mmmm, dried cod, how did you know?' added Sean, licking his lips and rubbing his belly.

They brought reindeer skin slippers for me, and Leif had brought a pewter cheese slice for Mum. He hadn't known she wouldn't be there. Trigve gave me a bright red ski-hat and Sean a thick blanket with polar bears on it.

'To keep you warm when I'm not here,' he said with a wink.

All four had filled their duty-free allowance with bottles of Aquavit, the Norwegian clear spirit.

Trigve put one in the freezer: 'Just in case we should decide to have a drink later,' he said with another wink at Sean.

After wolfing down Maggie's casserole we all made our way to Carran.

While the Norwegians reacquainted themselves with The Atlantic, Dad, Sean and I went to the internet café to discuss plans in more detail. We'd have to chase up our broadband connection and Sean, who mistrusted Dad's understanding of modern technology, insisted that he would sort it out. He emailed companies that might help the project and sent rough funding proposals to relevant universities and institutes. Dad stared out of the window with a faraway look in his eyes.

'Do you know,' he said to no one in particular. 'I feel like one of those artists who finishes their work and then throws it away.'

'Dad, what do you mean? This is your project.'

'No, I'm not worried. It's wonderful. In fact I'm overjoyed that you're all taking over. I can be the old caretaker who changes the light bulbs.' He laughed but didn't look very happy. 'Bring the busloads of children and drunken biologists. It's what I built it for.'

'Liam, are you sure now, about this?' Sean looked at me as Dad was still staring at the sea through the window. 'Have you changed your mind?'

'Dad, it'll be great,' I interrupted. I couldn't think of anything better than having the house full of people. And if I did go off to university or away somewhere with Ronan, Dad wouldn't be alone.

'As long as I get an hour or two in the tower, I'll be grand. Carry on, you've my blessing.' He got up and wandered out. 'I'll be in the pub,' he added.

'He's just worried about the change,' said Sean. 'And he's missing your mum.'

'She hardly ever wants to speak to him when she phones me,' I said, and I told him about our herring conversation. 'Let's carry on. It'll be good for him.' I was determined to bring some life into our old house and was confident that Sean would make everything ok. And the thought of getting broadband and satellite TV was much too exciting for me to be worrying about my dad.

'He'll be grumpy but he'll adapt. He always does.' I sat next to Sean and looked expectantly at the screen.

When we finished in the café, we made our way back towards the pub. I wondered if Cait was in town. I'd hardly seen her since she'd glued herself to Joe. We hardly ever travelled back from school together because she was always at Joe's house and though she asked me along, too, I really didn't want to be a gooseberry. Also, they spent time with the Kelly bitches and other friends of Joe's that I didn't really like.

Tom was often with them when he wasn't too busy with the farm. I supposed it would do him good to meet a girl. Cait told me he liked Niamh Kelly and I had felt nothing. There'd always been a warm feeling of security with Tom giving me his attention but all I could think about now was Ronan.

I had a permanent aching obsession about the fact that he hadn't contacted me since the last trip. Donal was always coming up to the house, why didn't Ronan ever come, or at least give him a message for me? It was as though he'd dumped the dogs on me and that was all he'd wanted. It was out of sight, out of mind with him. Even the driftwood seal was beginning to feel insubstantial as a guarantor of love.

Thinking these miserable thoughts, I trailed behind Sean to the pub and peered in to see if my dad was there. He hadn't arrived yet but the sight of Trigve staring back out of the window cheered me up and I went in to join them.

The guys all made a big fuss of me and insisted that I join them for a drink. I relaxed into the banter and laughed when a pair of arms encircled me from behind. I assumed it was Sean giving me a cuddle and nearly fell off my chair when a familiar voice said,

'Hello, green eyes.'

I felt excited and terrified all at the same time. When Trigve gave a wolf whistle, Ronan released me and started walking back towards the bar, watching me as he did so.

'Come with me,' he mouthed.

'Where are you going?' I mouthed back.

'I've to unload some stuff for the pub, will you come and help?' Ronan looked straight into my eyes and I couldn't speak but nodded agreement. We left through the back door to cheers and more whistles from the merry crowd around the table.

'Donal says there's a session up at your house tonight now that the scientists are back. We've to put some lobster aside for your dad and take it to Bridie's for her to cook. This lot's for the pub.' He pointed through the back door of the car at a container of lobsters and a lidded box of fish.

'Here, you take the mackerel.' He passed me the polystyrene box and heaved the lobsters onto the floor. I looked away from the desperate creatures and swore to myself that I'd never eat one again. It was hard to reconcile Ronan's love of animals with his casual attitude to sea life. Pushing that thought away I followed him into the pub. He'd grown more of a beard and his hair was longer. I was dying to run my hands through it and wondered if we'd get a chance to be alone later.

# 34: THE CURRACH

We dropped the lobsters at Bridie's and left the van there.

'I've something to show you,' Ronan said. He led me down the steps from Bridie's house onto the sandy beach at the far side of the pier. I followed, grateful to be near him and not caring at all where he was leading me.

'It's such a calm day, I wonder would you like a boat trip?' He was looking at a black hump that was nestling amongst the seaweed and driftwood below the dunes.

'A currach?' I asked.

'It's that one from the island. It was full of holes and problems but I managed to fix it up. I came over in it early this morning.'

Though it was scruffy looking, the currach was evidently seaworthy, as it had brought him from the island. He'd given it a fresh coat of tar to strengthen the old canvas covering, but inside the boat had been patched with bits of what looked like sticks held together with baler twine.

'It'll do for now and I've plans to work on it more.' He smiled down at the black boat. 'My mother's father and uncle used to make their own currachs. I remember, when I was little, watching them with a bubbling pot of pitch, fixing up the canvas. They used horse skins back in the day.' He stared out at the sea. 'The tide's with us. We could get to the island and back before the session.'

I couldn't have cared less about getting back for the session. To be rowed to the island by Ronan would be a dream come true. And I even had the thought that if I were destined to drown with him in his makeshift boat it would be a fitting outcome. In any case, my mind was far more preoccupied with what might happen once we reached the island.

Together we carried the canvas boat to the sea and climbed aboard. I nestled into the stern end and happily watched Ronan as he expertly rowed the little black boat away from the coast. The journey was quick, seeming to take no longer than it did in Donal's boat. A group of seals watched from the flat rocks on the north side of the beach as we approached the jetty. There was little movement in the air and, apart from the regular waders peeping and stabbing along the wet sand, no birds to be seen.

'They'll be out west, there's always a good run of mackerel on this tide.' Ronan didn't expand and I accepted his knowledge as a given.

'Will we go and look at the gannets?' I asked.

'Ah no, we'll leave them in peace. They've all got chicks now. You'll be out with Sean to do a count soon, I expect, now that Trigve and the others are here.'

Ronan had done a good job persuading Sean to leave the hatchlings and him in peace, but that would be over now.

I felt nauseous with nerves at the thought of what might happen as he took my hand and walked up the shingle strand towards the old house.

He'd been busy. The holes in the roof had been repaired and the door no longer creaked open on one hinge. It still felt like the inside of a barn but the tarp had gone and he'd made a cosy nook for sleeping and storage. The kitchen area had moved up to the fireside and he'd fashioned a slab of driftwood into a narrow table. The grate was empty and dampness pervaded the old stones. I clutched my coat to myself.

'I'll get the fire going.'

'Don't worry, I'm fine,' I lied.

He turned to me and spoke: 'Hello, green eyes,' he said again, pulling me close.

At first I buried my face in his jumper to hide my embarrassment at his tenderness. When I looked up his eyes were impenetrable, an opaque sea-swell that could drown my world.

He pulled me towards the bed and in a daydream I let him kiss me and begin to undo my buttons. When I shivered, he pulled blankets over me and stroked my face. My stomach clenched in fear and anticipation. I'd dreamed of this moment for so long but somehow had never got farther than the kissing bit. I felt just like I did in the falling dreams where I had to relax and let myself go otherwise I'd wake with a shock. I didn't want to wake from this. My mouth was dry, my jaw clamped with tension, and my heart seemed to have stopped beating.

When we'd warmed up a bit he slowly undressed me. I wriggled out of my jeans and shivered as his hand moved up my thigh. I hid my face in his hair and instinctively pulled him close.

Feeling exposed I said, 'You can, you know, take yours off too.'

He undid his belt, and then he pulled my hand to his crotch.

'You undress me' he said, in a deep, raspy voice. I closed my eyes and gently undid his buttons, all the while aware of what I was releasing. It was the first time I'd felt a man and though it was shocking, there was something vulnerable about him. It made me smile, this urgent thing that reminded me of a baby bird, all blind need and powerful insistence.

We turned towards each other under the blankets. He was so warm and his hot musky smell filled me with desire. All my expectations made me nervous, but the way he took his time and kissed me and muttered things into my neck relaxed me. He told me I was beautiful and looked into my eyes until I couldn't feel where I ended and he began. And then we made love. At first it was awkward. He fumbled with the condom for ages and I didn't quite know where to put myself. I'd been expecting it to hurt but it didn't at all, just felt odd and unfamiliar. It was like body surfing, when you catch the wave and let yourself go. And then it came easily to us. We fitted together so well. It was perfect, the way we became part of each other. All my fears of not knowing what to do melted away as my body answered his.

Afterwards we lay entwined and I stretched and would have purred if I'd been able to. I nestled into him, grinning with my accomplishment. I naïvely thought that it meant he was mine. But then he sat up, reached for his jeans and rolled himself a cigarette. He blew out a long plume of smoke and turned to look at me.

'Time to go,' he croaked and then he started to get up.

'Don't go. Please, not yet.' I pulled him back but he sprang up again. 'Hey,' I added. 'Come back here,' I wrapped my arms around him. He was really tense. 'What's the matter?' I begged.

'I always fuck things up,' he groaned and let his head fall against me.

I didn't speak and slowly his body began to relax. I could feel him give little shudders as his tension eased. At last we lay quietly and I tried to make sense of his change of mood.

All that mattered was his not leaving my arms. The smell of his slightly greasy hair, and our sweat mingled with the rubbery scent of the condom. I felt my heart thumping and realised that he must be feeling it, too, with his head pressed to my chest and his eyes firmly shut. I didn't dare interrupt him in case it made him get up. Instead, as he'd told me his dreams on the cliffs, I told him mine and then when he didn't speak I lay still and tried to relax with him in the dying light.

He suddenly leapt up. 'Damn! It's getting dark, we'd better go back.

I'd almost dozed off and jerked awake as he pulled his clothes on and was out through the door within seconds. I dressed as quickly as I could and stumbled after him. He marched through the shingle to the currach and I ran to keep up, tripping and twisting my knee as I did so. A surge of emotion made me hide my face to stop him seeing my tears. He indicated for me to get into the currach and pulled away from the shore without a word.

# 35: SWIMMING IN THE KELP

A southwesterly breeze blew us back to Carran. The going was choppy and it made me feel sick. I looked towards the horizon but the wind was so cold I had to sit with my head bowed as he pulled the currach through steepening waves.

'There's rain on the way,' he said with a grim expression. He hadn't smiled since leaving the cottage. He wasn't even looking at me. I couldn't fathom what had changed. I regretted telling him my dreams. They would've given him the message that I thought about him all the time. Too much, too soon, maybe I'd frightened him away. I bit my tongue and together we rode the tide home to the mainland.

'Hey, look!' I shouted above the wind. A grey seal's head had appeared in the water at the harbour mouth. She stared at us as we passed, turning to follow us with her gaze. He didn't comment.

He turned away from the harbour, towards the strand where the boat could be safely stowed. Faint red streaks showed through the clouds and I felt quite chilled after the journey.

'Come on, we'll get the van.' He walked in front of me without waiting. I tried to take his hand, but it had gone before I could reach it.

'Hey, what's the matter?' I asked again. He didn't answer. I couldn't believe how different he was from when we'd left for the island. 'Hey, Ronan!' I was angry now. How could he treat me like this after what we had done?

He turned and I saw sorrow in his face, shuttering of his eyes.

'I'm sorry,' he said. That was enough to set me off crying. The enormity of the day with its final disappointment crashed over me like a cold wave. I regretted what I'd done, I needed my mum and I wanted to get home. But then he touched my face, tracing my mouth and cheekbones, and then he held me, which made me cry all the more. He didn't say anything to explain his behaviour and I didn't want to press him. The kiss he gave me there on the beach reassured me that he still desired me. I tried not to think too much as we walked hand in hand to get the van.

By the time we arrived home it was dark. The moon and stars were hidden in low cloud and black tree limbs danced in a freshening breeze. The comforting fragrance of turf smoke gusted from the kitchen chimney: Dad must be in celebratory mood. That was a relief, hopefully he wouldn't realise how long I'd been gone. And it boded well for later on.

We walked into a scene of adult debauchery. Sean squashed up against Trigve, laughing hysterically at a rude innuendo from him. The other Norwegians, Donal and Martin were locked in a noisy debate about the EU and fishing quotas. The empty beer bottles might have had something to do with this well-fuelled fire, as might the half-empty bottle of vintage whiskey that Dad only brought out with a flourish when he was already half cut.

The first person to register our entrance was Bridie. She stopped what she was doing and pierced us with her steely eyes. I looked down to avoid her gaze.

Dad pushed his chair back.

'Clare, where have you been?' he said with the chill of unexpected anger in his voice. 'Ronan, how are you?' he added as a conciliatory afterthought.

My heart sank as everybody went silent and turned to stare at us. I wondered for a moment if somebody had seen us and reported my de-flowering to the world. But, no, how could that be? Or did he have some kind of parental ESP? No, surely not my dad. Mum would have been a different matter but then she wasn't there.

'I was worried, love,' he said in a quieter voice. 'Donal thought you might have gone out in the currach.'

All the while Bridie stared at us and I was convinced that she could see the state we were in. She looked from me to Ronan, and back again. I swear she even sniffed the air to pick up our shameful scents. Oh, why hadn't I just phoned to say I was staying with Cait? How could I have been so stupid as to come back home?

The atmosphere changed again when Ronan told them I'd been helping to tidy his fishing gear and clean out the van.

'And we had a little play in the currach, didn't we, Clare?'

'Yeah, it was fun,' I said, trying to sound sincere and normal.

Bridie looked sideways at Donal who nodded thoughtfully. But then, after another lingering, knowing look she started bustling around the range.

'Well, as it happens, you're just in time,' she said. 'The lobster's all gone but I'm frying up your mackerel, Ronan.' The table was littered with the bright remnants of four lobsters whose shells had been scoured clean. Bridie hugged Ronan. 'God, you're half frozen. Come and sit in by the range.'

Sean jumped up and shook Ronan's hand.

'Welcome, my man, sit down and have a drink.' Ronan agreed to a beer, but looked mortified at the attention he was getting. I imagined he'd rather be with the piping birds and dog-eyed seals on the island. He distracted himself by fussing with the dogs. Amber recognised him and came out of hiding to be petted.

Dad pulled out a chair for me. Our eyes met for a moment and I saw that he didn't have a clue what I'd been up to. He'd only been worried about my safety.

As Sean noisily cleared away the debris from the lobster feast Trigve stood up, clapped his hands and said, 'Shall we?'

He went to the freezer and produced a bottle of the icy fire that is Aquavit. Then, as Bridie slapped a platter of sizzling mackerel in the centre of the table, everybody clapped and cheered.

In my new glowing state I happily snuggled between Ronan and Sean. I felt for my lover's hand under the table. He squeezed mine back and reached for his beer, while Dad beamed at us and proposed a toast:

'To my beautiful daughter,' he said. 'And to the mighty mackerel.'

The Norwegians added their well-practiced toast to the herring: 'king of the sea.' Then Sean drank to Team Gannet. I caught Ronan's eye and pretended to sip the disgusting glass of Aquavit. He accepted another bottle of beer from Sean and acknowledged my look with an imperceptible nod. We helped ourselves to bread and mackerel, stuffing down the salty sweet flesh with appreciative groans, then stood in unison.

'Is it ok if we go to the tower, Dad?'

He nodded and eagerly resumed another round of toasts.

We walked through the back door out into the soft night. Dad cheerfully ignored us but I could feel Bridie's eyes burning an icy hole into my back.

We sat under the glass dome listening to the rain. I told him my most secret thoughts and he stared through the dark into my face. Before long we kissed and when we were sure of privacy we undressed. Sometime in the night, I woke and held him close. He was in deep sleep and didn't stir at all. I sensed a change in the darkness that meant dawn was on its way, so I pulled blankets over our heads to blot out the light. I fell asleep breathing in time with him, desperate to keep him with me for as long as possible. When I woke in the morning, after dreaming of him, he had gone.

*In the dream, Rowan stoops over a long piece of willow. His grandfather is showing him how to bend it into the framework of a currach. A seal with big green eyes watches from the shallows and he tells his grandfather that he must go. He wades into the sea and follows the seal down to the seabed. He lies smiling up through waving seaweed at the million spots of rain hissing on the surface.*

*I'm flying with the gannets. Hanging high in the sky we close our wings and plunge into a jade wave. The other gannets swim for the surface to grab at fish. I swim down until I find myself deep in a kelp forest. Swimming through the tendrils I see him playing with the seals. They turn somersaults and hang upside down, suspended in the kelp. I join them and then we're naked, coiling round and round each other, becoming one swirl.*

# PART THREE
## FLEDGING AND LEAVING

# 36: DUBLIN

Maggie and I took the train from Galway to Dublin where Mum would be waiting at the station to take us up to Nuala's house. We chatted for a while about the horses, the lambs, and about Cait who had been planning to come with us until that morning. The pub, short-handed, had called her and she'd jumped at the chance to see Joe, who'd be working there.

I'd been fed up with my supposed best friend for a while. She seemed to have dropped everything for Joe, including me. I hadn't even had a chance to tell her about my momentous afternoon on the island with Ronan. As the train rushed past fields and mountains, Maggie, who'd been up since six, closed her eyes and drifted off to sleep.

I moved from her side to the window seat opposite and gazed out watching the countryside for signs of life. I'd been looking forward to the catch-up with Cait. We'd have so much in common now. Lots to compare and discuss. I'd been out the island twice more. Once when Dad was away to Galway for the day, and once with Sean and Trigve, who turned a blind eye. Ronan and I had sneaked away to the cave on the black beach with nobody but the seals to see us.

It was a relief to find that Ronan had lost his reserve and took every opportunity to pull me into his arms. When he came into Carran with Donal, we met after school to walk on the beach. I was surprised no one had said anything about my chin that was red and raw from contact with his rough bristles. Gradually, as our inhibitions melted we relaxed into an easy familiarity.

So, as the train made its way towards the city I daydreamed about my man. Missing him desperately, I let myself float over memories of our times together. Nobody else on that train could have been loved like I had been. I couldn't imagine anybody would have discovered the depths I'd been to with Ronan. No other man on the train was as beautiful as him and I sighed with the pain of our separation.

The train juddered and rolled into the station. There was Mum in a dark blue coat. She looked smaller than usual, lost and vulnerable in the crushing throng of travellers. I held back while Maggie ran up to greet her. As Maggie moved away she turned to hug me.

'Clare, love, how are you?' she said.

I suddenly felt scrutinised. Mum never missed anything. I was sure she'd sense the change in me and felt exposed, as though she could smell Ronan on me. Probably she could. She always did have a nose like a dog. Oh well, I was one of the grown-ups now. I'd *seen the wolf*, as Mum liked to say about girls she suspected of having lost their virginity. Maybe she and Maggie would let me join in on those conversations they had. About the mediocrity of the beloved and how you end up despairing of the man you love. That didn't seem possible to me where Ronan was concerned.

We caught a taxi to Nuala's and sat in the kitchen drinking tea. Seeing Mum in a strange place made me notice her in a new way. She looked tired and pale and was trying really hard to be nice to me. I sensed her walking on eggshells around me and I don't know why but something in me did want to punish her for disappearing so abruptly that morning after the party. I couldn't help blaming her for Dad being so miserable.

But I supposed she felt guilty for abandoning us and I'd never have got away with my relationship with Ronan if Mum had been around, so I took a deep breath and tried to see things from her perspective. I returned her unnerving grin with a smile. She looked relieved and her face relaxed.

'I'm so sorry Cait didn't come, love,' Maggie said to me for the twentieth time.

'It's ok,' I answered again. It wasn't ok, though. It was awkward. If Cait had been there, we could have gone around the shops and left the others to themselves. I suddenly felt hurt that she'd let me down. Was this what happened to friendships when men were around?

'Granny's looking forward to seeing you, love. We'll visit her in the morning. I thought this afternoon we could maybe go shopping together.' Mum always knew how to cajole me. Shopping in Dublin was a rare treat.

'There's that new bookshop with the café, just round the corner,' Nuala said. 'Why don't the two of you go there? Maggie and I will do the dinner.'

Mum looked gratefully at her and turned to me. 'They've a brilliant stationery section, too.'

I couldn't help smiling. Mum hadn't forgotten my love of new pens and notebooks. During my childhood, she and I had spent many a rainy day choosing books and pens from remote bookshops in small fishing towns while Dad was off doing his field research.

When we got there Mum mentioned Ronan, asking if I was seeing much of him. Dad must have told her, and I knew from Cait that Mum and Maggie phoned each other regularly. I longed to talk about him and for the first time in my life had a glimpse of my mother as a woman. But I didn't, and could only blush and nod my head in embarrassment when she told me to be careful. She looked exhausted, probably from all her care of Granny, but I couldn't help wondering: had she found someone new in Dublin or did she still love my dad? I was relieved that she didn't make more of the fact that I had probably lost my virginity but was strangely offended, too. Did it mean she couldn't care less?

When she took my arm in hers, my instinct was to stiffen and pull away. Then, remembering that I wasn't a child anymore, I softened and let myself feel the warmth that was coming from her to me.

We chose my new stationery and then sat in the café, both avoiding relationship talk. Instead we discussed my career options. I told her that even though I had a conditional place to do marine biology at Cork, I was quite interested in history. Specifically the history of the islands, I thought, but didn't say. Maybe I shouldn't follow Dad's science route but apply next year to do history or even literature. Even as I spoke I knew it was all just a show for Mum. Academia in any form didn't interest me in the slightest. All I cared or thought about was Ronan, but I didn't mention that to her. She suggested that I not study yet but take a gap year and do some voluntary work abroad. I nodded with forced enthusiasm as she talked on.

'Don't do what I did, Clare,' she said earnestly. 'Don't limit yourself until you're really sure what you want.' She squeezed my hands until I returned her eye contact.

'I won't, but Dad keeps saying university is the only way forward.' It occurred to me that I might have an ally in Mum and that there was no point in hiding things. And I remembered that she was the last person to be judgemental. She'd drummed her liberal ethos into me from childhood. So I decided to take her into my confidence.

'Actually mum, I have been seeing Ronan. I've been seeing him quite a lot.'

Going back on the train I was glad I'd told her about Ronan. She'd given me the lecture about safe sex, and I managed to reassure her that I was a sensible grown-up now. And she asked me to come back and stay a while in Dublin after my exams but said she understood that I might be too busy at home. The thought of being away from him was unbearable to me and I spent the journey home daydreaming about falling into his arms as soon as I could.

# 37: BROADBAND

As May progressed, apple blossoms had turned into little hard green prom-
ises of the fruit to come and I tried to concentrate on the last of my deadlines.

I found out from Ronan that my interfering father had asked Donal
to tell him to stay away until after my exams. I was angry and told Ronan
to ignore him, but he said the fishing season was in full swing and that he
didn't have much spare time, anyway. Sean informed us that by mid-June
the chicks would be well grown and then my work for him would start in
earnest. Until then I should concentrate on my revision for my last exam. It
seemed that everyone was conspiring to abandon me to my utterly tedious
work.

Dad wasn't happy when I told him I might have a gap year and do
voluntary work abroad. He told me that I must keep to my plan to go to
university in October. I argued back but without much conviction. I really
didn't have a clue what I wanted. My only interest was Ronan.

'Even if you take a year out, it doesn't mean you have to fail your exams.
You won't want to be repeating the year,' he warned. 'You could accept a
deferred place and spend the year working with Sean, you'll get a great
advantage for your marine biology.'

'But Mum thinks I should take my time deciding. I don't know what I
want to do,' I countered.

'All the more reason to do well now,' he said. 'Then you'll have the
choice, won't you? Your mother doesn't realise that if you want to do sciences
you can't do it in bits and pieces, like an arts subject.'

These discussions usually ended in squabbles and I missed Mum and
wished she would come back and talk to him. Since the visit to Dublin, I felt

close to her again. And after our broadband connection arrived, we'd be able to Skype each other whenever we wanted, which would be brilliant.

The noise of tyres braking in the gravel on the drive had Sean and me jumping up and running out to see a blue van pulling into the drive.

We ran up the tower stairs.

'Dad! The broadband men are here!'

Dad frowned at the invasion into his daydreams as we came bursting through the trapdoor, but soon smiled gamely when our enthusiasm got through to him.

After some drilling and banging and a lot of running up and down the stairs, the tower was fitted with broadband. I was thrilled and Dad admitted that he was pleased at how easily he could now keep up to date with all his colleagues' work. It was so much easier than sitting in the café for hours every week.

It was also great news for the Norwegians. They were able to communicate with home and the search for funding continued. Silver-tongued Sean, who was not short of impressive scientific credentials, managed to create such a vision of educational magnificence that pledges began to trickle in

Every day I stared out at the island willing Ronan to appear. Of course it was too far to see him but I imagined him there waiting for me, or was he forgetting me? Anxiety increased as I counted the days until I'd see him again. Sometimes I considered ending the relationship before he did, but I knew I wouldn't be able to do that. It was an addiction and I was powerless to stop it.

By the middle of June, when the woods and banks were spotted with foxgloves and the exams were over, I looked forward to my first visit back to the island. Waking before dawn with a gasp of terror I managed to catch the tail of a dream before it disappeared.

*Ronan is standing on a cliff. He's facing north and has a black dog at his feet. I run towards him, knowing he'll stop me with a big hug. I throw myself into his arms to find that he's vanished and I'm falling. Dropping like a stone down towards the sea that seems to be miles below.*

I snapped open my eyes and tried to breathe my thumping heart into calmness.

The dream was so real. Had he decided to leave me? What did dreaming about a black dog mean? It felt like a warning. I told myself it must have been an anxiety dream. My greatest fear was that he'd changed his mind and was fed up with me. We'd walked Carran beach only five days earlier, and had had a long session of kissing in the dunes, but I hadn't been to the island for nearly a month, and I had a feeling of jealousy about it. As though the island was his true love, and I was a temporary thing. I wouldn't have dared make him choose between us, because I knew he wouldn't have chosen me. Once again I considered finishing the relationship, but he was irresistible to me. I could no more have left him than leave myself.

# 38: PUFFIN

Dad drove us down to the harbour in Carran. While Sean and Trigve climbed onto *Saoirse*'s deck, I told him that I might be staying the night on the island. He stared at me in speechless confusion as I blushed bright red.

'Have you asked your mother?' he said, with an embarrassed cough.

I started to protest that I was nearly eighteen and I think we were both grateful when Sean interrupted us to say that it was time to go.

*Saoirse* pulled away and I heaved a sigh of relief as we set off for the island, leaving Dad standing on the pier scratching his head.

'So, Clare, your exams are finished?' Trigve asked. 'You did well?'

'I've no idea, but at least it's all over,' I told him.

Sean came over and pressed mugs of coffee into our hands.

'Now we can really begin, Clare,' he said. 'We need to do a proper count of adults and chicks. The newly hatched are the black squabs. The older ones will be big, white and fluffy. Then in a few weeks we'll see them losing their down, until by the end of August they'll all be fully fledged in their speckled juvenile plumage.' He looked at me to make sure I was paying attention.

'Is it only me making the notes?' I didn't want that responsibility.

'No, we all work together and back up each other's findings. It's important not to miss anything. You and me, your father and Trigve, and if we get stuck we'll drag Leif and the others away from counting their herring. We can't all be here all the time anyway, so on a day like this it's not so bad, but on some days it might be only you and Ronan.' He winked at me and I couldn't help grinning at hearing his name spoken out loud. I couldn't wait for those days.

'Today I'll work with you and you'll get the hang of how we make the records.' Sean smiled and added: 'I believe we'll make a first-rate field researcher of you before the summer's over.'

I smiled, clutched the warm coffee and gazed happily out towards the island. At long last, school was over, forever. I was part of Team Gannet, and best of all, Ronan would be waiting for me, and hopefully he'd ask me to stay the night. A cloud covered the sun and as I zipped my jacket up to the neck, the memory of the dream reappeared and a sense of uneasiness returned to undermine my spirits.

As Donal turned *Saoirse* in to the quay, my fears melted away. He was there. He came walking down the shingle, one hand occupied with holding his jacket and a roll-up at the same time. The other hand held a thin stretch of blue rope. At the end of the rope was a large black dog. Ronan had a big smile on his face. His face, which looked so dark and grumpy some of the time, really opened up when he smiled. I sighed with relief, seeing him so relaxed and cheerful.

He caught the mooring line and then put out his hand to help us disembark. I had brought a bag of overnight stuff, which I'd felt awkward about, in case he didn't want me to stay. I needn't have worried because the first thing he did was give me a long kiss and tell me how much he'd missed me. Ignoring the *get a room* comments from Trigve, I kissed him back and then looked down.

'So who's this?' It was a pure black sheepdog. I presumed it must be the father of Tom's puppy.

'I never did find him, but he found me. He started coming up to the door after the other two left and I've managed to bring him in. He's tame now but I can't let him loose because of the ground nesting birds on the northeast slopes. That's probably where he's been living. He's been getting fat on plover and puffin chicks. He must have been lonely out there on his own. So he came to see me.' Ronan bent down to give him a scratch.

'Have you a name for him?' I asked.

'No, well, I can't keep him on the island. We'll have to find somewhere else for him. But we'll call him Puffin for now as he's so fond of eating them.' He looked down at the dog and ruffled his ears.

Sean lectured him about making sure the dog was gone soon and then we made our way up to the cliffs and stacks, having locked Puffin in the house.

As soon as we reached the top, the temperature dropped. Although it was a bright day, the wind sucked the warmth out of everything. Above and below the cliffs, the air was alive with birds. Gannets flew back and forth between their nests and the fishing grounds, while guillemots exploded like fireworks out of the cliffs. A motley crew of herring gulls and an Arctic skua searched for victims to harass. Their laughing screams filled the sky. Sean suggested shelter behind a hummock where we could settle down to take the census. Ronan pulled me into our wind shadow and breathed warm air down the back of my neck. Meanwhile, Sean was trying to explain where all the ticks and numbers had to go on the forms he'd printed out.

'I'll have to separate you two if you don't behave,' he snapped. 'Come on now, let me see you taking this a bit more seriously, now.'

It was so unlike Sean to snap that I'd momentarily forgotten how important the project was to him. So feeling suitably chastened I pulled away from Ronan and got to work. At the end of the afternoon we agreed that there were twenty-three chicks with parents in attendance. On a nearby stack at the edge of the colony a cluster of darker birds squabbled and shoved each other around. Sean explained to Trigve that this was our club of juveniles, prospecting for possible nest sites for the future. The four-year-old males were displaying to attract passing females to the stacks. There were certainly outsiders flying past the colony, giving its inhabitants the once over with beady cast-down eyes.

'They're up here for the fishing,' said Sean. 'But you never know, they may decide to come back here next year. We can't say we have a colony unless the birds do come back next year. Anyway, so far, so good, let's go back down the hill because I, for one, am starving.' He stood up and was almost blown over by a gust of wind. We'd only been there an hour but were all chilled.

'Jaysus,' he said. 'Let's go, lads.'

As we walked down the hill, I took Ronan's hand in mine and told him I was planning to stay the night. He dropped my hand and put his arm around my shoulder.

'I've been missing you and I've things to show you later,' he said.

I laughed. I'd been hoping for that.

# 39: AISLING CLARE

After waving goodbye to *Saoirse* and her crew, Ronan pulled me along the shingle in a rush to get back to the house. I assumed he must be eager to take me to bed until he whistled up the dog to come out with us. I hurried after him.

'I've been fixing up the currach,' he said. 'Do you fancy a spot of fishing?'

He didn't wait for an answer but led me down to the barn where Amber and her pup had been living. He'd turned the place into a workshop and in the weeks since I'd seen him he had re-made the currach.

'My dad gave me this.'

He handed me an old cloth-bound book. The pages, though mildewed with age, clearly depicted drawings and design notes for a variety of Irish currachs.

'I've decided it's an Aran Island currach. Though I think the design is closer to the County Clare type with the flared sides, maybe smaller.' He looked apologetic.

'Sorry, I've lost you there,' he said.

'No, no, it's really interesting,' I said. 'Go on, I want to know.'

'Right. So, I've fixed up all the rotten wood with hazel strips and I've replaced the old canvas with sailcloth. It's tarred with a mixture of pitch and coal tar, in the traditional way. Anyway, what do you think of her?'

'She's the most beautiful thing I've ever seen.' I looked in wonder at his creation.

The black body was smooth and as shiny as a ground beetle. The wooden innards had been polished until they shone and between the ribs of the boat, two seats had been built with a set of oars lying across them. What moved me the most though was the name of the boat. There, painted in white letters on the bows, *Aisling Clare,* which I knew was the Irish for *Clare's Dream.* As he stood, proud of his creation, my love for him deepened, but so did my fear of loss. He might have named the boat after me, but in a funny way it felt as though it was a substitute. I kissed him, desperate for reassurance. He laughed at me, telling me we'd plenty of time for that later.

We carried the lightweight boat down to the shore. Once seated, I tried without much success to have a go at rowing. The currach felt very light in the water and it was difficult to gauge correct pressure for the oars. After five minutes of struggling I lifted them from the sea and let Ronan do the work.

The tide was low and though it was bright daylight, a stilling of the air suggested evening approaching. Puffin sat in the bows, looking out to the horizon with his ears flying out behind him as though he'd been born for the sea.

The half moon rose over the mainland and already an evening star was showing itself above the island. Though the wind had calmed, the sea had not and I felt a flicker of fear as land disappeared behind swell. The black boat seemed insignificant and fragile on the ocean. The seaworthiness of cur-rachs is world famous but that didn't stop me worrying that a wave would come to sink us. Ronan made his way round the headland, towards the black beach. As he entered the bay, the swell flattened and the boat steadied.

'The land shelves a bit here so we'll try for some fish.' He dropped a line into the water. I relaxed. I could swim to shore from here and anyway the sea seemed calmer in the bay.

We weren't the only ones fishing. First one, then another, then half a dozen round heads popped up out of the water. I laughed as Puffin barked at the seals.

'Shusssh, hush now.' Ronan pulled him in from the edge. 'He went in over the side the other day and I'd a job getting him back.'

So Ronan had done this before. I didn't like to think of him out alone on the sea with no one to help if anything went wrong. I said nothing and trailed my hand in the water, looking at the beautiful seals while Ronan caught his fish.

There weren't many birds and the seals must have already eaten because they seemed more interested in playing than fishing. Ronan managed to bag three good-sized pollock and then decided to call it a day.

'We'll walk home from here, I'm thinking of leaving her up in the cave. It's a better place to fish from.' He manoeuvred the currach sideways to the shore and told me to jump out. Together we carried her up to our cave. The place we'd first kissed.

Fine drizzle accompanied us on the walk back and I shivered with the chill of it and with anticipation of my first whole night on the island. An hour later, as adult gannets were returning from fishing with crops bulging, Ronan placed a plate of sizzling pollock fillets in front of me. The smoky musk of turf smoke clouded the room.

'I must see to that chimney,' he said.

'Shame you can't live here permanently?'

'Maybe I will though,' he said, gazing into the fire. 'At least I'll stay until someone tells me to go. And if this centre starts I could become a caretaker sort of thing.'

I felt myself grow small.

'What about me, Ronan?' I didn't mean to say it out loud and instantly regretted my clinginess.

'Maybe you'd like to come and live here, too,' he said with a half smile and a shy flash of his eyes. 'I've missed you.'

'Even if we could I'm supposed to be going to university. But I was maybe thinking of travelling first for a year. Would you fancy that? Going to South America or Africa or somewhere to work on a project?' I tried to catch his eye but he seemed to have gone somewhere else. 'Or anywhere, would you not...?' My voice faded, he stared at the door and I regretted saying anything.

Eventually he turned to me and asked if I was ready for bed. Despite my insecurities we had a wonderful night. Lying in the firelight, listening to the sea as it rolled over the clattering shingle, I held him, sleeping, in my arms. His breathing didn't quite keep up with the sea and together they made a discordant rhythm that kept me awake. I kept perfectly still and let my mind wander over the possibilities for my future.

The weekend in Dublin had opened up all kinds of exciting things. Nuala and Mum had obviously been talking. They had a lot of contacts between them, and were eager that I should have a gap year. Going abroad to do some voluntary work had seemed like a great idea. We'd all sat round

Nuala's table, drinking wine and talking about the wonders of the world. Nuala was determined to help steer me towards a purposeful life. There were all kinds of conservation projects in amazing places around the world. Dad could help me join some turtle-breeding programme, for example. Or there was work to do in the many orphanages of the third world where children who'd lost their families to war or AIDS were desperate for help. Mum was most keen that I should work in such a place. Maggie had suggested that Cait and I go together as she didn't have a clue what to do either. Apparently the whole world was at my feet and Mum never stopped telling me how lucky I was to have so many opportunities. In my fantasies Ronan was there, too, sharing it all with me.

I had gone to bed that night in Dublin dreaming of adventures and new horizons. But now as I lay in Ronan's bed watching the last of the fire's embers fade to black, I knew that none of these things would happen for me. My soul had other ideas. Or was it my heart? Whatever it was, there was no way I'd ever leave the side of the dark man who was sleeping in my arms.

I would take a gap year at home. I could work at the tower and see where things went with Ronan. I knew that Dad would be happy enough to see me helping at the centre. Mum and Nuala would have to be content in the knowledge that I was planning to study marine biology and therefore the experience would be essential.

I'd tell everybody, even Ronan, that I planned to go to the Marine Institute. He mustn't know how needy I really felt. All I really wanted to do was to lie listening to the sea, forever safe in the arms of my island man. I sighed loudly enough to make Ronan growl in his dreams. Then I let myself be lulled to sleep by aligning my breathing with his.

# 40: SUMMER LOVE

July sported her leafy abundance. Meadowsweet, dog rose, wild honeysuckle and dancing fuchsia decked the hedgerows of the mainland. On the island, brambles pursued their conquest of broken walls and tumbled roofs with renewed vigour. Only Ronan's cottage boasted a clear pathway and he liked to sit there in a patch of sun by the old door, with Puffin at his feet. When he wasn't working with Donal he'd be fixing fishing gear or simply gazing out to sea, a roll-up smouldering in his hand. He rarely went to the mainland now. All he needed was brought to him on Donal's boat.

Ronan and I had been lovers for nearly two months but it felt like forever. I couldn't remember my life before him and I wanted, more than anything, to live on the island with him. Dad had other ideas, of course. He was wary of our relationship, hinted that it could ruin both of our lives. He agreed that I could stay there at weekends but that during the week I must fulfil my commitment to the project.

So I had to return with the others to process the data we gathered each day. Sean had asked me to take on secretarial tasks for the project. He relied on me to help him collate and report the gannet findings to the Institute. And, as he was still after funding for the Marine Centre, I helped him by proofreading his begging letters and checking through grant proposals. I enjoyed the challenge of it and as well as earning me cash, it meant lots of visits to the island.

Sometimes the weather was too rough and then I was unhappily grounded at the tower. This was just such a day. I knocked and then walked into Sean's room. He'd woken at six, taken one look at the lashing rain and jumped back into bed. Trigve was curled around him. I squeezed my eyes till they were almost shut, in case anything was on view. No, Trigve's blond hairy back was all I could see and Sean was almost hidden by his leonine companion.

'Ha. Clare. Come join us.' Trigve patted the bed next to him. Once I'd have blushed and looked at my feet. These days I felt able for such taunts and sat down heavily next to him, pushing him aside to make room. Sean yawned and sat up in bed.

'Hi, darlin',' he grinned at me. 'Y'all right?'

'Yeah but, you know, it's boring being stuck here all day. Dad's in a mood, he didn't even bother lighting the range before he went out.'

Sean reached over and patted my hand. 'He's lost without his Orla. You must be missing her, too.'

'Clare's missing that handsome man,' Trigve added. 'She's missing you know what. Ha ha ha.'

This time I did blush.

'Come in here, we'll keep you warm,' he said.

'Trigve, behave,' Sean said. 'Sorry, Clare.' He pushed Trigve down and leaned over him so that he was pinned and couldn't move.

'It's ok, guys. I'm going to make you lazy people coffee. Then I'm going down to see Cait. I'll be back later to do the emails if that's alright with you.' I got up and pulled the curtains wide open, causing them both to grimace at the light.

'You're like a couple of vampires, cringing from the sun,' I said. 'Except there isn't any sun. Oh, by the way, Sean, please can I borrow your car?'

'Ah, the real reason you are making us coffee,' said Trigve.

'Course you can, darlin', how about a bit of toast, too, then we won't have to get up till lunch time.' Sean snuggled back under the duvet with a groan of satisfaction.

In the kitchen I found Leif and the others eating breakfast. Leif had rekindled the fire and Dad must have walked the dogs because all three of them lay damp and steaming in their beds. The only signs of discord were the mewing cats that ran to me and began circling like hungry sharks.

'Oh ho, no one's fed you furry people,' I said to them.

'Oh yes, they have,' Leif said. 'Liam told us not to believe them if they said they were hungry.'

'Did you see him?' I asked them.

'He's gone out in the car to get things for a survey.'

I shrugged and began making the boys' breakfasts. The others made comments about how they never got breakfast in bed but I smiled. I was looking forward to seeing Cait for the first time in ages.

Cait opened the door and threw her arms around me.

'Where the hell have you been?' She looked at me carefully and took in my grinning face. 'My God, you look amazing. I've never seen you so glowing and sparkly. And you've gone all skinny.'

I was desperate to talk about Ronan and gratefully began telling her all about him.

'Yeah, I've been off my food. I love him. I just wish I could really know what he thinks of me,' I pouted. 'It's driving me crazy. Do you think I'm going mad?'

'Yeah, you definitely are. I was like that at first. Don't worry, it'll fade. You'll begin to realise he's just a waster like every other boy in town.' Cait spoke with feeling.

'Yeah, but he's not. That's one thing you can't say about him. Moody maybe, but ...' I realised she looked a bit down. 'Things not ok with you and Joe?' I asked.

'Yeah, well, Joe's a total mong. When he's not at work, which is most of the time, he's either surfing or getting high. Martin and Bridie would die if they knew. Oh yeah, and he's going round the festivals all summer. I can't afford to do that and Mum wouldn't let me anyway.'

'That doesn't mean he doesn't want to be with you, though. He probably thinks you've got plans of your own.' I reassured.

'I guess, but summer's looking bleak. And you're never around. Do you actually go and stay in that shack on the island?'

'Yeah, it's amazing. We lie in the dark, listening to the sea and the seals and everything. You'd love it. He cooks me fish that he catches. Oh, by the way, he's found a dog. We think it might be the father of Tom's puppy. How's he getting on with it?' I suddenly noticed how quiet the house was. 'Where's Spats?'

'Gone with Mum. Apparently it's supplies for some overnight survey you're all doing.'

'Really? News to me.'

'But Tom's puppy's lovely. Well, he's not really a puppy any more. He's worked really hard with him. He's good at rounding up the sheep already.

He'll be back later if you can stick around. He's bringing a girl from college.' Cait stood up and stared out of the window. 'God, look at that rain, did you get soaked walking down?'

'No, Sean lent me his car.'

'Hey, do you think we could take it to town?'

'I can't go on the main road unless Sean or my dad's with me.' I wandered over to the window.

'Oh, yeah, anyway tell me more about Ronan … if you want.'

Of course I wanted to. He was the only thing I wanted to talk about. 'The only trouble with him is there's no way he'll ever leave the island.'

'Shit, well, that might be ok. I can just see you, gathering seaweed to fertilise your potatoes, stirring the stew whilst your man's away fishing. Knitting for the six children and telling them stories of the Selkies.' Cait laughed but I didn't.

'Actually, apart from the six children bit I quite like that idea.'

'You'd go nuts, Clare. It'd be grand for a summer but you'd be lonely. And what would you live on? You can't really live off seaweed and mackerel you know. He's put you under a spell. Come on,' she said, jumping out of her chair. 'I've some new music that you won't have heard yet out on the island. My new phone can play it straight through these speakers. Tom sorted it for me. Time for you to join the real world, Clare,' she said.

I was annoyed with her. Why didn't anyone understand? 'Actually, we do have broadband at the tower and I've ordered an iPad online with the money Sean's paid me. And if you must know, I don't want to be an island woman. It's just that the sex is fantastic. I mean seriously awesome.' I grinned at Cait who raised her eyebrows comically.

'Fair fucks! God, I must go and find Joe today,' groaned Cait. 'It's been too long. He's quite cute really, considering he's such a dick. Shall we go to town later? Someone's got to be driving to the pub.'

'Yeah,' I agreed. 'I can't see that lot hanging around all day. Come up and have lunch with us, we can talk them into it.'

Although I was missing Ronan the idea of an afternoon with my friend, being silly and having a laugh was just what I needed. Ronan was my lover and my most beloved soul mate. But he didn't often make me laugh.

# 41: HERRING

When we got home Maggie and Dad were unpacking groceries from bags, putting some in the cupboards and some into boxes, which they stacked by the door. I had a peak inside.

'What's all this for?' I asked. Dad stopped what he was doing and told me all would be revealed up in the tower if I'd like to make my way there. Cait followed me up and when we'd all assembled Sean told us about the forty-eight-hour survey.

'We've to find out how much the chicks are eating, which means that between us we need to keep watch around the clock. Not during the hours of darkness, but dawn and dusk are important times so we'll be staying on the island. We've to work out how many trips to sea the adults are making and what the frequency of feeds is.' He counted heads. 'We've got you, Clare and me, Liam, Trigve and Ronan. Leif will be joining us, too. We'll do watches of two people for four hours at a time.' Cait looked crestfallen and for the first time I realised she probably felt as left out of my life as I did of hers.

'Maggie and Liam have bought the supplies so we've only to wait for decent weather and we're off.'

'Where will everybody sleep?' I asked with some trepidation. Cait giggled. I wouldn't be able to share Ronan's bed with my dad snoring a few yards away.

'We'll all be staying in the house,' Sean said. 'We've camp beds and there are sleeping bags for everybody. That way we all stay warm, dry and well fed.'

Nobody but me seemed to care about the intimate sleeping arrangements.

While Sean showed us how to collect the data I daydreamed about how I could get Ronan to myself, imagining us making love in the cave. Dad seemed very upbeat about it all and talked incessantly about night field research he'd done before with a friend of his from Galway. Taking sound recordings of nightjars in clear-cut forestry down in County Clare had been the worst.

'When it wasn't lashing with rain, you were getting bitten to death by the midges.'

'At least there'll be no midges on the island. It's too windy,' Sean said.

'Can't promise there won't be rain, though.'

We spent the rest of the afternoon around the kitchen table. Trigve got out the Aquavit to toast the survey. Before too long they were drinking to the herring once more. Cait and I were just about to go up to my bedroom when Donal dropped by for a visit. He told us that the Aquavit toasting must have had an effect because the herring had arrived.

'There's a great bloom of them, from down by the mouth of the River Shannon, all the way up to Donegal. For this year at least, nobody will go hungry.' He accepted a beer from Dad. 'It may not last all summer but they're here now for a while.' He raised the bottle to his lips and smiled in satisfaction at the table thumping and cheers that greeted his news.

'That'll give us an easy start to the survey. But we'll have to repeat it when the fish have gone. One oily fish doesn't make a summer.' Sean popped open a beer and raised it to his lips.

'Slàinte Donal,' he said.

Cait decided to stay over and we spent our night in the tower. It was two in the morning when we wobbled up to bed. Lying under the dome we chatted and laughed for another two hours. Apart from analysing the fact that Donal had given Maggie a lift home, we had our own relationships to discuss. Since our last sleepover we'd both grown up. No more giggling about stupid boys and annoying girls. Instead we shared shy confidences about the mysteries of love and the fear of losing it. We fell asleep yearning for our boys but happy to be snuggled up with each other under the dome. The pattering rain lulled us to sleep and I prayed for good weather so that I'd see Ronan in the morning.

# 42: THE FORTY-EIGHT-HOUR SURVEY

I woke with the sun in my eyes. The dome glowed in the morning light and I lay for a while watching the creatures glittering in the glass frieze. I nudged Cait who was lying on her back open mouthed and snoring.

'Hey sleepy, I've got to get up and go. You stay on a bit if you want.'

Cait groaned. 'It's not fair. I want to come with you. What's the weather doing?'

I stood up and stretched my hands up towards the dome and spun around from window to window.

'Well, it's not raining but it does seem windy. Oh, please God, I hope we can get to the island. I feel like I've forgotten what Ronan looks like.' I grinned at Cait, who raised her eyebrows back.

'Look at you. You'll never be able to focus on the gannets. I hope you've got condoms,' she said. 'Wouldn't want you to give birth to a seal pup.'

'You, too, friend, wouldn't want you giving birth to a mini-surf-dude. Come on. Breakfast! I'm starving,' I pulled at her blankets. 'I'm sure you could come with us you know, if I ask my dad.' I hadn't spent time with Cait and Ronan at the same time. It would be strange. 'What's Joe up to?'

'Probably busy with his bros.' She hooked her fingers into air quotes to emphasise the word. 'Which means he'll be watching football and getting high.'

I felt sorry for her, at least Ronan wasn't into getting wasted all the time.

'I'm getting into surfing, though; in fact you should come with us some time. It's cool, I'm quite good actually.' She smiled and writhed her body into a surfing posture with arms outstretched. 'Oh, well,' she sat up and rubbed her eyes. 'At least he's not shagging anyone else.'

'Well, the surf might be up today. If you don't want to come to the island, we can drop you into town when we go.'

'Yeah, that'd be cool.' She jumped up and started dressing.

'Ronan likes Joe, why don't you both come out and stay with us next time he's got a few days off.'

I knew it was a fantasy. Two couples having a romantic summer break on an island. What was I thinking? Ronan would hate anyone else coming to stay in his cottage, even his old buddy Joe. He didn't seem to see any of his friends anymore. The island had taken him away from all of us. Sometimes I even felt it was a strain for him to have me there. And I knew that he didn't really think of us as a couple. At heart he was a loner. Because I loved him, I was helpless to do anything but accept his distance. I often felt as though I was trying to tame some wild creature that might bolt if I moved too quickly.

She smiled at me and agreed.

'Camping with you on the island. Wow! This is going to be the best summer.'

We found four sleepy Norwegians and two grumpy Irishmen propped up in various states of hangover around the kitchen table. Dad drowned his with a gallon of tea while the others sipped strong espresso.

'Right. Who's for bacon and eggs?' I was keen to get to the island early, in case the weather changed for the worse. Ignoring the moans of protest, Cait and I set about making a huge fry-up that was consumed in minutes.

Sean stood up and coughed politely. 'Right lads, we need to get our skates on. The wind's dropped and there's no reason why we can't all be at our posts by lunchtime.'

We all piled into Dad's car and went on down to the pier where Donal waited. Under a cloud of herring gulls that had followed a fishing boat in, *Saoirse* chugged away from Carran onto a bumpy sea.

While Donal went below to organise fishing gear, Dad took the helm and the others crowded into the wheelhouse for coffee. As soon as he'd handed round mugs of Trigve's bitter espresso, Sean began his instructions for the forty-eight-hour watch. He and Trigve would take the first watch to get a gist of the situation while we all set up camp. I was relieved. I'd have time to see Ronan. The problem was that my dad and Leif would be there, too.

But perhaps we'd have a chance to visit our cave for some time together. My stomach turned over at the thought of getting him alone again.

The sea picked up movement as *Saoirse* left the shelter of Carran Bay. By the time the little quay on the island drew near, the waves had white caps and the milky blue water had turned to oily green petrol. Gannets sailed back and forth. Against a greying sky they looked unnaturally white, like photographic negatives. I searched for the familiar form of Ronan on the quay, straining my eyes in the hope that he would suddenly pop into view. The beach was empty. Not even an oystercatcher strutted along the strand.

The cottage door was closed and no smoke trickled from the crumbling chimney. No black dog wagged its welcome. No dark man hunched against the wind with his roll-up sending smoke signals to me.

# 43: THE BLACK SAIL

The boat bumped its arrival and jolted me from my distracting search. Donal helped with unloading and then turned to us.

'Well lads, I'm away now. I'll call in tomorrow morning in case you need me but otherwise I'm gone.'

'Where's Ronan?' Sean asked what I was thinking.

'Ah, he'll be away fishing. The winds picking up so I expect he thought he'd go early. Perhaps you'd tell him from me that I won't be needing him tomorrow, so he's grand to stay with you folk.'

'Thanks Donal, you're very good to us.' Dad said. 'Would you bring me *The Irish Times* when you come back? I might just have time for the cross-word.' I rolled my eyes. The forty-eight-hour gannet survey seemed to have already lost its allure for Dad. He hadn't spent a night away from the tower for ages and perhaps the reality of being out under the blustery island skies no longer excited him as once it would have done.

'Don't worry, Liam, we will keep you entertained.' Trigve winked and pointed to his rucksack where the lid of an Aquavit bottle was peeking out of a side pocket.

'Jesus, Sean. Don't let him near me with that. It'll be hard enough to stay awake on watch without the icy spirit.' Dad put his hands to his head. 'To be honest, I've a headache after last night.'

Trigve pushed him playfully but Dad just gave him a scowl. I decided to keep away from him for a few hours. He was even grumpier than usual when he had a hangover.

While the men stood about exchanging insults, I walked up towards the old house. I was vaguely aware of *Saoirse*'s engine starting up and looked over my shoulder in time to see her pull away round the headland.

Ronan had cleared more brambles from the paths and the doors and windows looked oiled and robust. This was more than a summer camp. I could see that he really did mean to live here. Sean came up behind me with a large food box.

'Open the door for me, would you,' he said. 'Where the hell is Ronan? He's getting paid for helping us on this.' He pushed past me and dropped the box onto the table with a sigh of relief. 'Mind, I suppose he wouldn't have known we were definitely coming now. Fair do's,' he added. 'Fish for dinner!'

'One of these days we'll be able to get a signal,' I said to keep the mood light. 'Then we'll know where people are.'

'Can you see Ronan or Donal with a mobile phone? I don't think so, darling.' Sean laughed and I had to agree that he was probably right.

'Could he not get radio contact like Donal has on *Saoirse?*' I suddenly realised what a great idea that could be for us.

'Well, he could, Clare, but would he want to? Anyhow, the weather here's been mixed. He probably thought he'd take his opportunity while he could.'

'He'll have gone out fishing in his currach.' I remembered our first night on the island, and a pang of yearning made me sigh out loud. Even though it all made sense, I felt frustrated and let down by him. There was no time to think about it as the others arrived with the gear and we all set about making camp.

Dad elected himself fire monitor and I found myself turning to the kitchen supplies. It was all comfort food: milk, bread, butter, eggs and bacon, and enough biscuits to set up a shop. Not a fruit or a vegetable in sight, unless you counted jam. I stacked our dairy goods in next to some milk of his, in a stone recess beside the back window where it was always cool.

'We'll head on so, see how our chicks are doing. We'll be back around four and then we can start the watch proper. We'll eat together after dark when the birds are asleep.'

Sean and Trigve, nodding their goodbyes, made their way out through the door. I looked at Dad who was on his knees trying to get the fire going, and at Leif, standing in the doorway. I had to get away. This wasn't how it was meant to be. I had to find him before I went mad.

'I'm going for a walk if that's ok. I'll come back and help make the beds up in a while,' I said.

'Are you, love? Right so, don't be long,' said Dad. Leif nodded and smiled and moved aside to let me pass. I walked to the black beach, where there was no sign of Ronan or the currach. I then decided to go and join the boys, hoping that from the top of the cliffs we might get a glimpse of the currach.

Sean and Trigve sat huddled from the wind in a hollow behind the cliff edge. Below them a few gannets were returning home from fishing forays, though many were still out. For the most part, there was little movement in and out of the colony.

'It's siesta time,' said Trigve. 'I'll get some shots of the whole site, shall I?' He began unpacking camera gear and attached a new lens to his camera.

'That's a big one you've got there. Oh, and I like your new lens,' Sean said.

'Har har har, you're very funny,' Trigve quipped back. 'Yours is bigger than mine though.' He nodded suggestively as Sean unleashed a telescope from its casing.

'Wow, I didn't know you had all that,' I said.

'We've had some funding through from Norway, thanks to my friend here, did I not tell you?' Sean screwed his telescope onto the tripod.

'I got mine for the Svalbard project and I can use it until they ask for it back.'

'He's good at that, Clare, watch you nail your furniture down.' I laughed at the thought and at Trigve who was pretend-grappling with the telescope.

'Hey look, Trigve,' I pointed him to a nearby rock where a cluster of mottled juvenile gannets was huddled.

'They look like three year olds,' Sean said. 'You can see how the plumage is losing a lot of its darkness.' Trigve began photographing the youngsters, stopping to fiddle with the camera after every third shot. He was very pleased with his new toy and joyfully showed us the results after a few minutes. Sean was more excited about the young gannets.

'This is what we need. If these come back here next year and join the breeding pairs we'll really be in business.'

'Look at that one.' Trigve had seen something else through his long lens. On the far side of the colony a mature gannet was displaying to any birds that passed over.

'He's showing off,' Sean explained. 'He'll certainly be back next year and hopefully a female will have noticed what a great nest-site he has. This is how it all starts, Clare.'

I smiled and nodded, momentarily cheered by his enthusiasm.

The next hour was spent counting and photographing every bird. Most of the chicks had lost their baby fluff and seemed far too big to be sitting on their nests

'They're thinking about the sea.' Trigve voiced what was in my mind.

'Yes, I think we picked a good time to do this. Another month and some of them will have fledged and gone.' Sean, having counted his charges, now let his telescopic gaze scan the oceans. 'With all the herring about we might see dolphins, or a Minke whale.'

'Hvalblast!' Trigve yelled suddenly and then remembering we were supposed to be quiet he put his fingers to his lips: 'Shuusssh,' he whispered. 'It means, Whale ho! That is what the whalers shout where I come from.'

'Let's not go there, Trigve. We don't approve of whaling, do we now? He's probably been at the Aquavit, Clare, don't mind him.' Sean pointed our attention back to the gannets.

None of the birds were fishing close to home. Maybe the herring had moved offshore again. As he followed the progress of two small local trawlers that were motoring out to deeper water something else caught his eye.

'Hey. Look at this.' He moved away to let me look through the telescope. 'Is that what I think it is?'

A small dot on the western horizon evolved under the magnification of the glass, into an almost cartoon-like spectacle.

'He's a long way out. Following the fish probably.' Sean laughed.

'That's not something you see every day,' he added. 'A currach with a sail.'

Ronan had erected a small black sail onto the bow of his boat. It billowed out in an offshore wind and the currach was making impressive progress away from the coast. Ronan, who appeared to be wrestling with the sail, was turning the boat away to the north.

'Herring for our dinner, I think,' said Sean.

Trigve prepared his camera for a long distance shot.

Through the telescope I could see every detail. It was a pretty sight. The black boat and its silhouetted skipper were at one with the sea. They surfed effortlessly through the peaks and troughs of Atlantic swell. Puffin crouched under the sail with his nose pointing north. His sheepdog senses may have been confused by the smell of the sea but with his ears blowing in the breeze he made a fitting figurehead to the timeless image of a man in a boat out fishing.

We watched Ronan until he became a mirage and then a shimmer and then there was nothing to see. Trigve snapped a few pictures but to me they looked like the ocean with a dot on the horizon.

'He's following the herring home to my fjords,' said Trigve with another guffaw.

'I'd say it'll be a while before there's food on our plates,' Sean said. 'He'll have to tack round to the east before he can come in. I reckon he won't be home till six. Come on, let's go back, we'll send Liam and Leif for the first watch.'

I told them I'd like to do it instead of Leif. Sean nodded at me and told me not to worry.

We went down to the house, weighed with equipment and with news about gannets and fishing. I tried to ignore the terrible feeling that I'd never see him again. I put it down to my own fear of the sea and reminded myself of what a practised sailor he was.

# 44: THE WOODEN MODEL

I sat with Dad writing notes about the birds and drawing doodles of gannets and currachs in the margins. The wind was strong up on the cliffs and I had to constantly push hair back from my eyes. Evening sun purpled the sea stacks. A few gannets left for their last fishing trip of the day. The magnificent birds stood on the edge waiting for an updraft to set them flying. As their wings caught the breeze, they floated high above the land, turning flamingo pink for a moment in the light. In every nest, a parent stayed behind, napping with one eye open. Though the chicks didn't need brooding, they were at risk of attack from other adults and so had to be babysat. The youngsters seemed content to sit preening or intently watching the adults with their piercing eyes. They took in every possible scrap of information.

I scanned the sea for a glimpse of my fisherman lover. Dad said he'd probably approach from the north, which made me desperate to run to our beach and wait on the shore.

In between shifts I'd gone to his workshop just in case there was a message for me. It was uncharacteristically chaotic with abandoned tools and rejected pieces of wood strewn over the floor. Scribbled plans and roughly drawn diagrams were pinned to the walls, some circled, some crossed through. On the saw bench was a perfect copy of his currach, roughly a foot long and intricately precise with two little seats, thole pins and perfectly shaped oars. A carved miniature dog lay curled in the bows. Above the dog's head was a mast from which a square black sail hung from a single wooden cross spar. A rope secured it to a ring on the starboard side and I could see it would be possible to swing it easily to the port side. It looked improbable to me, but what did I know? I recognised the simplicity of the design and the beauty of the smooth black model. It fitted snugly into my arms and I cradled it, hoping for a clue as to its maker's whereabouts.

The sea cast ribbons of turquoise, indigo and milky green and the off-shore breeze blew tips off the breakers, creating rainbows of spray over guillemots bobbing in little black clumps at the foot of the cliffs. They were the only birds, fishing for sprats near the stacks. Every now and again one disappeared without a splash and popped up several meters away. A string of shags emerged from behind a rock, skimming the sea as they headed home for the night.

'No fishing here,' Dad observed. 'Everything's coming home from the northwest.'

'I wonder how they know,' I said. 'I suppose that's where Ronan's been, too.'

'Ah, he'll be heading back by now. He'll have to work hard, mind, against the wind,' Dad frowned. 'It's strange these winds we get nowadays. Whatever happened to our good old southwesterly gales? Still, it's great not to be rained on.'

We sat for a while longer and when the sun began to redden and sink towards the sea we stood and gave the sea one last searching sweep. Trigve and Leif came up to relieve us and sit in the gloaming hoping to catch the last few remaining gannets on camera.

When we arrived at the house Sean was there with tea and biscuits ready for us. No herring, no Ronan.

'I'll be back in a minute,' I said, walking out quickly before anyone could stop me.

Sean followed me out.

'Why isn't he back, Sean?' I felt sick when I saw the concern in his face.

He didn't speak but took my arm and together we made our way along to the black beach. The beach was empty. The seals were gone and even the cliffs appeared deserted of birds. It was almost dark. Where was he?

'Listen, love,' said Sean. 'He's probably had to pull in up the coast. These winds are all over the place and sailing the currach is an art. You really need somebody else rowing to steady the boat while the sail's blowing. I had an uncle who was a champion currach racer. You should have heard the arguments about how not to sail a currach. Ronan will show up with Donal tomorrow.'

'I hope his boat doesn't get damaged. It's like a part of his soul,' I said.

'True enough,' said Sean. 'It's the connection to his mother and the island.'

'He won't be able to stay here, will he?' I asked.

'I think it improbable. He's a great man to resurrect that boat, though. Come on, love. I'm down for the dawn shift and we need to sleep.' He pulled me gently away from the dark beach and we chatted about the moon and the tides, anything but Ronan, as we made our way back to the house.

I knew he was right. Ronan understood the sea and he'd have pulled in at one of the coves further up the coast. I'd have to be patient. I told Sean I'd do the dawn shift with him. Before bed Trigve and I climbed to the highest point of the island to try and get a signal from Sean's phone to get a message to Donal. It was hopeless. There was no signal. All we could do was wait and hope.

I did cover the dawn shift, carefully noting the figures Sean gave me. I'd not slept at all, but had lain in Ronan's bed listening to the wind. It seemed to be trying to tear the roof off the old house. All I could think of was my lovely man fighting the waves and sinking to his death. I saw the currach, cracked like an egg on the rocks and Puffin swimming desperately for a shore that never came.

# 45: THREE WEEKS LATER

I heard Mum in the garden, drinking her coffee and humming as she pottered about. Then Maggie must have arrived because I could hear them talking on the bench under my window.

'It's all overgrown, love. I'm sorry, I meant to get around to tidying it up for you.'

'God, Maggie, you've done enough for us these last months.'

'How's Clare?' Maggie asked.

'Well, she's still devastated, of course, but at least she's thinking about university again.'

'Oh yes? What will she be studying?'

'She's not at all sure but seems to be drifting towards her place at Cork, much to Liam's delight. Her exam results weren't great but it's a practical course and they seem pleased with her fieldwork. The gannet project has given her a few points.'

Her voice went quieter and I strained to hear. 'You know, to be honest Maggie, her heart's not really in it but Liam and I think she should get away from here. Meet a new crowd. Put the past behind her.'

I groaned and turned over. I couldn't imagine going to the shops in Carran, never mind moving to Cork.

'I'm going to get stuck into those weeds,' Mum said. 'Oh, it's so good to be back in my garden.'

'I'll give you a hand. I've to wait a while for Liam to get back. We need to discuss figures for the centre. How are you now, love? With him, I mean. I hope you don't mind me asking.'

I pricked up my ears when I heard them mention Dad: 'I'm very grateful, Maggie. He really is a new man since you got involved. You've a way of keeping him motivated. I'm sorry you had to pick up the pieces for me.'

'I was happy to help,' Maggie said. 'You know I love you both.'

'And of course I don't mind you asking. I should think you deserve to know.' Mum must have been weeding because she was breathless and hesitant and I didn't catch all of it.

'We still love each other … ' I heard her say. There was a long pause and I thought they must have gone, but then:

'I do love him, Maggie, but we did need this time to re-evaluate things. Perhaps all marriages need that once in a while. And now of course Clare's situation has made us see what's really important … I wonder, will she ever get over this? Come on, let's have some more coffee.'

Their footsteps receded and I felt nothing. Who cared if Mum and Dad were fine again or if the centre was a goer. Life was an empty nothing for me and for the first time in my life I thought about suicide. I couldn't sleep at night and I couldn't find the energy to wake up during the day. My only comfort was the little wooden seal, which I clutched to my chest every night, willing it to bring him home to me.

Turning on my side, I stared at the wall. And then I must have slept because I woke on my back. A breeze from the open window had blown my curtains apart. Dust motes swirled in a shaft of sunlight, settling on the model currach on my bedside table. I'd taken it from his workshop the day my dad and Sean had prised me away from the island.

When the boat didn't return we'd all presumed Ronan would arrive with *Saoirse* the next morning. There was nothing we could do but hope for the best. But then Donal turned up without him. We had to tell him the news that his son had vanished. Donal immediately radioed the coastguard and the searches began. I was worried but strangely calm, certain that he must be safe in a harbour up the coast somewhere. There was no body, no broken boat. Until I saw evidence I'd cling on to a shred of hope that he was still out there.

Donal became my partner in grief. I'd grown close to him and for two long weeks we'd created a daily rite of walking the cliffs and shorelines of Connemara. Despite the repeated efforts of the coastguard with their boats and helicopters, we had begun a ritual of getting into his battered car and trudging painstakingly along the beaches in all weathers. It seemed like an offering that the ocean gods might accept as payment for his return. Every day held bittersweet relief when we returned to Carran empty handed. Occasionally we spotted a dark lump lying in the shallows. It always turned out to be driftwood covered in goose barnacles or a mound of storm tossed seaweed.

Poor Donal. How terrible to lose his wife, and now his only child, to the sea. Bridie said that apart from his walks with me, all he did was stare out to the island. Everyone was worried he'd follow his family into the waves and made sure to keep an eye on him. At least Bridie didn't blame me. In fact she seemed sympathetic and I cried on her shoulder more than once. In the days following Ronan's disappearance, Donal's lobsters were left trapped in their pots while he took *Saoirse* trawling the coast for signs of the currach. He didn't trust the coastguard to do the job properly and wanted to inspect every offshore island and rock. He was still sending distress calls out to passing ships. Dad said he'd founder *Saoirse* on the rocks if he weren't careful.

I tried to drift back to sleep but was too awake to drop off. Now, twenty one days since Ronan's disappearance, I explored the dread feeling that he might be dead. Looking away from the little currach, I cradled my seal and cried into my tear-soaked pillow, tormenting myself with questions: How could he be so stupid? Did he not care about me? Why had he not waited for me to arrive before he went out fishing? If he'd really cared he wouldn't have gone. Maybe he'd drowned himself deliberately, isn't that what people said his mother had done? With a big sigh I crawled out of bed and opened the curtains.

Mum and Dad were sitting next to each other on the kitchen doorstep catching a few rays of sun. The weather had been glorious since the weekend but I hadn't the heart to go out into it. I waved down and Mum waved back. They both stood up and I saw how worried they looked. I had to admit that it was a relief they were both there. The day she came home, after Dad had phoned her about Ronan, was the first time I cried. I'd been wandering about like a ghost frozen in a nightmare, and then Mum had put her arms around me and I'd cried and cried and cried and didn't think I'd ever be able to stop.

# 46: FLEDGINGS

It was a lovely sunny day in late August, the three-month anniversary of my first time with Ronan. The ocean idly lapped the sea stacks and puffs of breeze buffeted the cliff top grasses into a shimmering dance. Their seeds blew away to start a new life and hundreds of tiny spiderlings flew with them, on filaments of gossamer, abandoned to their fate.

I was alone on the cliff on my first trip back to the island. Sean had insisted and I'd left him and Trigve collating data below in the house. His sheer enthusiasm had persuaded me and I was glad I'd come. One by one the fledglings had made their way to the edge of the cliff and jumped and I hoped to see it for myself. So far, nineteen of the nests were empty. Sean and Trigve had witnessed eight youngsters making the leap. One unfortunate gannet had jumped just as the breeze dropped and had plummeted to its death on the rocks below.

Gannets were brilliant parents but they ceased responsibility as soon as the chick leaves. The newly-fledged youngster had to take the leap and try to stay airborne for as long as possible. Then it would crash, legs splayed, onto the surface of the sea. The well-fed chicks would be too heavy to get themselves into the air again, so they started the long migration south to the African coast by swimming. After a week or two they'd have lost weight and could then flap away from the surface. The young gannets had to quickly learn the art of plunge diving to catch fish if they meant to survive the journey. Occasionally a chick was mobbed and drowned on the water by adults but nobody had seen it happen in this small group. The good news was that there had been a surge of late summer mackerel. The Atlantic was a soup of oily silver fish. Lucky gannets.

I was sorry to have missed the chicks being ringed. It had been quite an adventure for Team Gannet. All the Norwegians had helped, though Leif was the climbing expert. The gannets hadn't taken easily to their nests being invaded and had powerful stabbing beaks, so he'd had to wear protective clothing while he grabbed each chick to put a ring on its leg. Now, it was only a matter of waiting to see who'd survived and who hadn't.

The young gannets wouldn't return for three or four years but they might be picked up somewhere else along the coasts of France, Spain or Africa.

Eight had been seen to leave, ten more had gone without any human witnesses and one had died on take-off. There were four left and I willed them to leave while I watched. The wind was strong enough for a successful launch and I was glad that the sea looked calm enough not to drown a gannet landing for the first time in water.

They looked so vulnerable. Teetering on the edge of their nests, flapping new wings to build up muscle, they were at the mercy of fate. And, as I knew, fate could be very cruel. At least I had parents to pick up the pieces when I crash-landed. My young man had left the nest and drowned at sea as some of these gannets would. I felt for one optimistic moment that at least I could make a new life. Though gannets paired for life they would take another partner if they lost their mate.

As the afternoon wore on, the wind picked up and my knees and back hurt from sitting. I un-kinked my legs and was about to stand when I saw movement in the colony. The adult birds stopped their preening and resting. One after another they made their way to the edge and let themselves float up on the wind. Then, swooping down, they flew away, low over the sea, eyes down, looking for fish. In the midst of this, two of the fledglings tottered to the edge and began wing-flapping for all they were worth. I sat as still as possible, hardly daring to breathe. Could this be the moment I'd been waiting for?

One of them caught an updraft. Rising with feet askew it followed an adult and was gone, skimming the waves but managing to keep airborne. I didn't see it come down and hoped it would stay on the wind until well clear of the coast. The other young gannet stood flapping a while longer. It reminded me of someone on a diving board who keeps looking down and changing their mind

'Come on, come on, be brave,' I said under my breath.

And then it was away. This one didn't manage to fly far and landed in the middle of a group of guillemots that scattered, running on water, in all directions. The gannet preened for a while and then paddled away to the south. I sat watching its impressive progress until it had swum from view, then I reluctantly tore myself away from the last two youngsters, who looked settled in for the evening.

Walking down towards the cottage I thought about the two gannets. One had flown off without a backward glance and the other had struggled from the start. Of course the first gannet would eventually land and have to swim, and they'd both face their share of challenges. But the main thing was that they'd got away. They were fulfilling their destiny, whatever that held for them. As I came to the cottage, the familiar ache, a cold stone wedged in my stomach, hit me as I wondered what destiny had in mind for me.

# 47: SELKIES

Cait and I sat on Carran beach watching Donal reverse *Saoirse* away from the harbour. We dug our toes into the warm sand and sipped cans of fizzy orange.

'He was round again last night,' said Cait. 'I heard his car go this morning, I dunno why Mum doesn't just admit that he stays the night with her.'

'Really?' I looked at her with mock horror. 'He sleeps with her?'

'God, Clare, don't go there. He's nice enough but I'd rather not think about that.' Cait took another slug of orange. 'Anyway, when Tom and me have gone, it's good that she'll have someone around. I was a bit worried about her being left on her own really.'

I nodded as she spoke.

'Yeah, I know what you mean. I would've hated leaving Dad. Thank God Mum's back. And he's ecstatic that I'm going to Cork.'

'So good you got in,' said Cait.

'Yeah, but all I really want is for Ronan to come back.'

Her face dropped and I felt sorry to have brought it up yet again. Cait had been so patient, listening to my tears and sorrows. 'It's fantastic about you though. You're really lucky,' I said. Cait was going travelling with Joe.

'I'll come and stay in Cork with you when we get back though. That'd be really cool. It'll be great when you get used to it.'

'Yeah, I guess once I get used to it.' I forced a smile. 'We can go out if you come, explore all the clubs.'

'Brilliant, I could bring Joe. Oh, sorry.' Cait blushed.

'God, will you stop apologising. I don't mind you seeing Joe. Just because I'm a widow ... '

We stared out across the water. Donal's boat had disappeared around the headland. It was strange to see him back fishing. I'd wondered whether either of us would ever want to go to sea again. This was my first visit to the beach since the day Ronan showed me his seaworthy currach and rowed me to the island for our first lovemaking. I'd been so happy that day, little knowing the pain that was to come. I could have wept, thinking of my naïve younger self of only three months earlier. Despite my sadness I'd found myself breathing out with relief when Cait and I had taken our shoes off to run down onto the sand. Far from making my pain worse, I felt connected to Ronan here.

'It was good going back to the island again.' I spoke my thoughts aloud and didn't expect a reply.

Cait didn't say anything for a while, then she said, 'I knew Sean was bound to drag you out there sooner or later. You and your gannets.'

I smiled at that. 'Ronan's gannets,' I thought. 'Thank God he's living at our house. Trigve's staying for the winter, too, but the others are going back to Norway. Mum says it's woken the place up and that Dad's nowhere near as grumpy as he used to be.' I stood up and shook sand off my clothes.

'Come on! We've got to do it now before the sun goes in.'

I held my hand out to help Cait up. We stripped off to our swimming togs and ran tentatively into the cold water. A big wave caught us and with shocked screams we let ourselves be dragged under. We came up spluttering and spent the next half hour duck diving under the waves and body surfing. I hadn't laughed so much since before Ronan. I lay on my back in the green water, willing him to appear seal-style beside me. The cold stone of sorrow still sat in my middle but at least I was laughing again. Floating next to Cait in the water I faced a truth that I'd been pushing to the back of my mind.

'Cait,' I had to shout to get her attention. 'Cait, I need to tell you something.'

She turned a somersault and stood up, shook water from her ears and pushed hair back from her eyes.

'What?' she shouted back. A wave took her away and I'd to wait for her to come up again and shake more water from her ears.

'My period's late.' That stopped her.

'What the fuck, Clare, what do you mean?' she stared with mouth open.

'No need to swear, it's probably just the shock or something and I hadn't really been thinking about it with everything that's happened.'

We body surfed back to the beach and sat in the warm bath-like shallows.

'Have you done a test?'

I shook my head.

'We'll get one today. Why didn't you say something? How late are you?'

'I think my last one must have been back in early July when I think about it. So I've missed my August one and I think I should be due again now.'

'Whoa! ... What will you do if you are?'

'Mum and Dad will go ballistic but how can I not keep it? If I am pregnant, it's Ronan's baby.' I found myself prodding my tummy. It didn't feel any bigger than usual. 'Anyway, like I said, I'm sure I'm not. I don't feel sick or anything. It's most probably the shock I've had.'

'Yeah, probably. You've always been careful, haven't you?' She gave me a look. 'You have?'

'Well, yeah, but you know how it is? Once on the island, it sort of came off inside me. Do you know what I mean? I thought it'd be ok, though.'

'Fuck's sake, Clare, I thought you were a biologist. You should have known this could happen. It's not by magic, you know.'

'Shit! I know. I'm sure I'm not. I can't be. Will you come to my house and I'll get a test? Please, I can't face it on my own.'

We hauled ourselves out on to the sand like seals and seemingly without a care in the world stood dripping on the shoreline. And then Joe and Tom came ambling down the beach.

'Dude, look, it's a pair of selkies, quick, get their skins and we'll take them home with us.' Joe shouted to Tom and the boys picked up our clothes.

'You bastards,' we shouted as we chased them up the beach.

We called in at the chemist, where Cait got me a test, and the boys took us up to Maggie's. We watched Tom rounding up sheep with his dog and told him that the sheep looked miserable being constantly used for sheepdog practice. Joe asked us how we could possibly tell.

'I'm just gonna walk Clare home,' Cait said. The boys were used to me being needy and miserable lately and didn't bat an eye.

Joe was sitting by the fence rolling a spliff and hardly looked up.

'You're a total loser, Joseph Healey,' Cait said as we walked away.

On our way up the hill my stomach began to clench with anticipation. I didn't know what I wanted the result to be. Either way would be awful. If

I wasn't pregnant, I'd have lost the chance to keep a little piece of him. If I were, how would I cope? Babies were for other people. Other, much older people who had husbands and jobs and houses. Cait took my sweaty hand and squeezed it.

'Will we go and find Orla?' she said.

'No, if it's negative she doesn't need to know what an idiot I've been. And I don't want her telling Dad, he probably thinks I'm still a virgin.'

We went into the upstairs bathroom. Cait turned to the window while I did my life-changing wee.

'You look, Cait,'

I closed my eyes and handed her the test. She didn't say anything until I opened my eyes.

'Pull your knickers up, love, you're going to be a mum.'

She must have seen my face drain of life because it was a shock even though it was no surprise.

'Oh, sorry, isn't it good news? Are you going to get rid of it? We don't have to tell your folks. They'd never need to know … ' She sat on the bath.

'No, it's ok,' I said. I pulled my clothes back together and looked at my face in the mirror. 'Come with me, though.'

The kitchen was empty and the back door open. Mum leaned back on the step, while Maggie and Bridie sat like two chickens roosting on the old bench with their faces tilted sunwards.

'Girls, join us,' Mum said, standing to let us past.

Cait squeezed in beside her mum on the bench while I walked to the sundial and turned to face them as if I was about to give a recital. Cait and the three women looked friendly and expectant. It crossed my mind to wonder what they thought I was about to say. It certainly wasn't this.

'I'm pregnant.'

There it was. The news was out.

Mum stood motionless, mouth gaping.

'I don't care what any of you think. It's mine and I'm keeping it.'

I felt the arms encircling me. Mum's, Maggie's, Bridie's and Cait's. Tears fell as I let them hug me. They almost lifted me off the ground.

'Of course you are, love,' Mum said. 'Let's go and find your father.'

# PART FOUR
## RETURN

# 48: FIVE YEARS LATER

I lifted Aisling down to Donal who waited on the boat below. She ran straight into the wheelhouse and jumped on Sean, making him drop his bag.

'Hello, darling,' he said. 'Welcome aboard!' He picked her up and put her in the captain's chair. It was rarely sat in by anybody but visiting children and Aisling thought of it as her own.

'My grandpa says I have to be very quiet when you tell me to,' the little girl replied.

'And will we go for a swim later?' said Sean pointing at her rucksack.

'I'm wearing my swimming togs,' she giggled. 'But my mammy said I've to wear my wetsuit, too, to keep me safe from jellyfish and sunburn.' She looked at me: 'Is it true we might see the seals?'

Sean smiled at her. 'Your mammy and I have to count the gannets, and afterwards we'll all have a swim at the black beach. We might find seals there.'

Donal came in and started up the boat's engine. He ruffled Aisling's hair and gave her his binoculars.

'Now Aisling, you'll tell me if there are any dolphins.' He gave a signal to Dad who threw the mooring line down onto the deck and jumped aboard. *Saoirse* chugged backwards away from the pier and turned to head out of the bay.

The sea sparkled all around us and I sighed with contentment. There was no breeze to speak of and it was a beautiful day. It had rained most of April and May, but June had brought the summer and it felt wonderful. Dad's bones were achy with dampness. A few warm days would sort him out. I was pleased he'd come to the island with his granddaughter. She loved him, and he was the nearest thing she had to a father.

I'd almost decided to stay at home as I needed the time to get some work done. I should have been minding the centre and besides, I still found it hard to visit the island. Couldn't help watching for a black boat on the horizon. But I wanted Aisling to know and love the place her daddy had loved and it was such a gorgeous day. It was probably the last chance for a day off in a while. Earlier that day I'd taken bookings for almost every day the following week.

'Hello, Island Research! Clare O'Brian speaking.' I'd picked up the handset and listened carefully to the caller. It was June Garrigle from the school in Clifden. 'Yes, that's fine. Ok, next Tuesday at ten. Wait on Carran pier and the boat will be there.'

I had scribbled down the details, replaced the phone and filed the booking. I liked having school parties to organise. The money was good and the kids were always so enthusiastic.

There was a knock on the open trapdoor.

'Hi love, brought you a coffee. Whew, it's hot in here, isn't it? Do you want some air?' Mum put the coffee down and began wrestling with the windows that were stiff from not having been opened for some time.

'Thanks Mum, I tried to open them but they're jammed solid.'

'I'll send Tom up. He's down helping me in the garden. He's desperate to earn a bit of money so I've got him for the morning.'

'They haven't started haymaking then?'

'Your dad and Sean will give them a day tomorrow. They're going to break the back of it then. I said we'd help Maggie with the food for them.'

'I can't really leave the phone, Mum.'

'But Clare,' she said. 'You used to love the haymaking and I don't like thinking of you cooped up here all day when it's so beautiful outside. And I'll mind the phone today. Sean's insisting he needs you on the island. Take Aisling and your dad, it'll do you all good. I'll mind the fort.'

Minutes after she left Tom came clattering up the stairs. A visit from somebody my own age was rare. Donal had moved in with Maggie the year after Ronan disappeared which meant I was practically related to Tom and Cait through Aisling, who was of course Donal's granddaughter. Cait was studying to be a farrier.

She was in her element, working with horses and travelling about the countryside in her own little van. And she'd dumped Joe, which was sad for them but a relief for me to have my friend back for a while. And Tom was my other best friend. He'd stopped pursuing me when he saw how heartbroken I was over Ronan. He became the loving older brother I'd always wanted him to be and an uncle to my darling Aisling too.

Aisling was born on a full moon in May. Mum and Maggie held me through the labour and helped me with the baby. I was still broken hearted over Ronan but my dark little Aisling changed me in ways I could never have dreamt. It had never been in my plans, of course, but she gave me something to live for. As she grew bigger, I grew stronger. It was hard being stuck at home with a baby when my friends were travelling and going off to festivals but it had given me a little piece of Ronan. During the pregnancy I lay with my hands circling the writhing bump of my belly, imagining myself giving birth to a seal pup with Ronan's eyes. It was a big surprise when her eyes turned a rich sapphire blue. She may have been her parents' child but she was very definitely her own person. Rather than inheriting Ronan's introverted ways or my shyness, she came into the world roaring and determined, my beautiful Aisling.

# 49: THE SEAL

Sean and I sat at the table in the cottage writing up his notes. The old stones were damp after the wet spring and we both wished, not for the first time, that Ronan were still here to keep the house warm. After he went no one had the heart to visit the place much. However, on a lovely June day, with shafts of dusty sunlight pouring in through the open door, it was a handy place to make notes. The bed had long gone, and all other reminders of our time together had been all but taken over by the brambles once more.

The gannet colony had grown. The second year had been disappointing. Twelve pairs from the original twenty-three had returned and a large club of young, non-breeding gannets attended the colony. Of the twelve eggs hatched, only eight got away. Sean was much more circumspect about ringing and examining birds after that year. He feared the disturbance had caused one pair of adults to abandon its chick.

In the third year, presumably some of the juveniles from the previous years' clubs decided to nest. Ten pairs, thought to be from the original twenty-three, nested again but another thirteen new birds attracted mates and successfully hatched chicks. All in all, twenty-one fledglings got away. Around one hundred and twenty non-breeding gannets also attended the colony.

In the fourth year, forty-four pairs nested on the stacks. Unfortunately, an awful summer of storms and high winds damaged a few of the nests. Several chicks died falling onto the rocks below. However, a record thirty-one youngsters swam away to the south and several of the first year's brood were seen roosting at the edges of the colony and prospecting for nest-sites.

This year, Sean was dancing with glee, literally, when we found that eight of our original chicks came back to breed on the island. The colony had grown to eighty breeding pairs and there were now several hundred juvenile and non-breeding birds. We had a colony, and I grieved that Ronan couldn't see it. Or maybe he could. I sometimes fancied that he lived secretly with the seals on the black beach.

The good news was that our research centre would continue to be funded. The island had been declared a sanctuary and nobody was allowed to visit unless they were authorised to do so by Island Research. Visiting ornithologists and marine-life experts as well as groups of tourists and school parties could book through the centre to visit the island. We sometimes organised catering for these visits, usually just coffee and sandwiches after a trip or soup if the weather was damp. Dad and Trigve had mounted an amazing display of photographs and facts about the life cycle of gannets, mackerel and herring of course.

We finished the report and picked up our bags.

'Shall we?' he said, offering me his arm.

We made our way along to the black beach. The afternoon had grown still. After the cool of the cottage it felt hot outside, and I tentatively touched my nose to feel for sunburn. The sun was such a rarity that nobody bothered much with protection from it. Sean took off his shirt, revealing pale skin.

We climbed down the gully onto the beach, smiling at what we saw. Aisling, resplendent in her pink and blue wetsuit, stood in a rock pool. Dad leant over her, pointing at something. She threw her head back and laughed her outrageous chuckling laugh. Her hair, in two high bunches, flew up behind her as she held her arms up for Dad to pull her out.

'Mammy,' she shouted. She ran away from her grandpa towards us.

Sean, who was in the middle of taking off his shoes, lurched sideways as she bounded into him.

'Oops,' she said, nearly knocking him flying. 'We saw a hermit crab and Grandpa said it wanted to move out of its shell into my wetsuit.' She laughed again. 'Will you swim with me? He said it's too cold and he won't let me go on my own. Please, please, please.'

'Yeah, I can't wait,' I said. 'Let's go now while it's nice and warm.'

Aisling screamed with delight and pulled me towards the sea. Sean sat with Dad and said he'd come in when I'd had enough. Aisling would want to stay in for hours. Small breakers lined the black beach but the bay was sheltered and a safe place to swim on such a lovely day.

The green water looked inviting but was very cold. Aisling seemed oblivious to the temperature but I gasped with shock as I dived headlong through a wave. I picked her up and threw her onto the next one. She swam away from me like a tadpole, then, turning to lie on her back she said she'd a game to play.

'We have to pretend to be seals. Both of us have to just have our heads out and we have to stare at each other without talking or laughing. The first one to laugh has to be pushed under the water.'

So, sitting on the seabed, submerged apart from our heads, we stared at each other. After ten seconds Aisling couldn't contain herself and she laughed. I pushed myself up out of the water with a big splash and grabbed her.

'Come on, it's too cold for me to stay in.' I ran up the beach with her onto the warm black rock-slab where Sean sat.

'Look!' he said, putting his finger to his lips.

I turned round to see that a seal's head had appeared in the sea, not ten yards from where we'd been swimming. Without hesitation, Aisling ran back down the beach and into the waves. Sean and I ran after her.

'Leave her, she'll be fine,' he said, standing in the shallows. I don't know why I stood there and didn't race right in and grab her. The seal seemed to have disappeared and Aisling looked around, trying to see where it had gone.

Then I saw it, a dark shadow in the water, travelling at speed towards my precious child. What was I thinking? I waded in to reach her, tripping over a submerged stone and falling forwards onto my belly.

'Clare! For God's sake, go after her,' Dad shouted.

I scrambled to my feet and stood transfixed as tears brimmed over my cheeks.

She bobbed in the water, laughing and crooning to the seal. Its big head was cradled in her arms and she was talking to it. 'Where's your mammy?' she said. 'Are you all lonely?' The shiny dark eyes looked up at the little girl and its nostrils opened and closed. It stayed for a few moments more, allowing itself to be stroked and cuddled. Then, gently and slowly it sank from her grip and swam away out of the bay.

Sean picked Aisling up and put her onto his shoulders. We watched as the seal turned one last time to look back at her. Then it was gone.

On the boat trip back, Aisling begged Sean to take her up to the bows. She scanned the sea desperately hoping for another glimpse of her seal. Donal looked at me thoughtfully.

'She takes after Eimear,' he said to me.

'What do you mean?'

'Eimear was very fond of those seals.'

He left Sean at the helm and stood outside, looking back at the island. I followed him out.

'Aisling reminds me very much of the island woman I married. I remember her standing at the bows, her black hair blowing in the wind,' he smiled. 'You know, Clare, I've never said it to you but I feel at peace when I see the child. She's Ronan's daughter and Eimear's grandchild, an altogether unexpected blessing on my life. Wouldn't you agree, Liam,' he shouted in through the door to Dad, who nodded and came out to join us.

'She reminds me of your mother, Clare,' Dad said. 'Did I ever tell you, Donal? I met Orla at an anti-apartheid rally. There she was shouting her head off and waving a banner. I fell for her instantly, never dreaming that now, thirty years later, I'd be standing on a boat watching her granddaughter at the bows staring at the sea with that same determined smile.'

'I wonder what Ronan would have made of her?' I was cautious in front of Donal but felt it might be a safe moment to mention the taboo subject.

'I often wonder that myself,' Donal answered. 'If only he could have seen her, he'd see his mother in her and himself, too.' Donal smiled and went back in to the wheelhouse. We were approaching the bay.

Aisling ran in from her wildlife-spotting vigil with Sean. 'Can I drive now?' She climbed into Donal's chair and pretended to press buttons and look over her shoulder as he turned the boat into Carran harbour.

# 50: HAYMAKING

Bright sunlight backlit the dancing fuchsia, and honeysuckle scented the warm air. Bees journeyed from flower to flower, re-fuelling on nectar and filling their pollen sacks. A light breeze ruffled the hayfield and we all watched while Tom turned the baling tractor. His sheepdog sat upright beside him with its paw on Tom's arm.

'Donal, do you remember?' Maggie said. 'When we did it all by hand with the hayforks and old Fearghus.' She smiled, recalling the big horse.

'I do,' he said. 'You used to help the Healeys with the hay, I remember seeing you then and thinking what a cracker you were.' He laughed and kissed her.

That would have been back in the days before Cait and I were born, and well before either of them had married. Neither could have known then of the heartache and loss that was to be their fate. She'd lost a husband, he a wife and a son. But now they had each other and that was good. I envied them when she took his strong hands and told him how soft they were under the calluses. She pulled them around her waist and put her arms around him. Did they know how lucky they were to have found love so late in life? I felt sad thinking I might never have those feelings again.

'Come on, let's go and see if he needs a hand,' Donal said. As they walked down to the far end of the field, I said I'd go back to help with the food.

Mum sat at Maggie's kitchen table preparing sandwiches for the workers. Cait squatted with Aisling on the floor where together they were playing pulling games with Spats. He growled and tugged for all he was worth while the girls pulled his rubber ball-on-a-string away from him.

'Brilliant, you're here at last,' Cait said. 'Careful he doesn't nip you,' she turned back to Aisling.

'He won't,' she said.

'He will if you wind him up,' I answered.

'There's all the sandwiches done now,' Mum said as she stacked the packets into a cool-box. 'Have you finished the flasks?' She looked at Cait.

'Yep, they're in that rucksack. Let's go?' Cait lifted Aisling, who nodded then screamed as Spats jumped up after her.

By the time we reached the hay field, the men were stacking bales onto a low loader. Maggie walked over to join the women.

'We'll take these bales over to the barn before we stop,' said Tom.

'Ok, We'll set up the picnic by the river.' Maggie shouted back to him.

The sweaty men appeared just as Mum finished laying out the food.

'That's great,' said Tom. 'We should get it all in before the evening. Hopefully the rain will keep off till then.' He helped himself to a sandwich.

'Our Norwegians are coming back at the end of the week,' Dad said. 'We could all have a barbeque for the summer solstice if it stays fine.' He looked at Mum, who smiled and nodded back at him.

I liked Dad's new sociable self. Whether it was having Aisling around or having the centre up and running, he was a different man these days. Mum had changed, too. She seemed to have found a balance, doing journalistic pieces when she had the chance and working on a play. And she loved her garden. The nagging dread that she and Dad would separate had faded away.

'We've a couple of monkfish tails in the freezer,' said Maggie, smiling at Donal who kept her well supplied with fish. 'We'll bring it up to your kitchen for the barbecue.' She pulled Aisling onto her lap and asked her what she'd like to eat.

'Can we have sausages, Auntie Maggie?' Aisling replied.

'She doesn't mean the barbeque,' I laughed, and passed her an egg sandwich.

'Eat up, lovely, we can have a swim when our lunch has gone down.'

After our sandwiches we lay in the grass to rest. Maggie, Donal and Tom had been up since dawn and we were all sleepy in the sun.

A big splash sent spray onto my face and woke me from a half sleep.

'Sorry, mammy,' shouted Aisling from the river.

'She's a little mermaid,' Maggie said.

I leaned up on my elbows and laughed at the sight before me. Cait was lying on her back in the water and Tom was about to throw Aisling onto her. She screamed as she hit the water and completely submerged. Then I saw a bubble trail as she swam away and popped up by the bank.

When I jumped in she climbed onto my back and we swam up river pretending to be an otter and her cub.

'We'd better get that hay into the barn,' Tom said. The men walked to the barn where the low-loader stacked with hay waited for them and we women went back to the kitchen. We stopped on the way to see the horses and then Maggie took us in to see her lambs. Aisling was entranced with the black lambs and Maggie told her they were all the descendants of her black ram, Snowball.

'Your mammy nursed him when he was a baby,' said Maggie.

Aisling knew all about Snowball but she liked to ask about him every time she saw the sheep.

'I've got to go back to the centre to check the messages,' I said.

'Can I come with you? I want to look at something,' Cait asked

'Anything to get out of the washing up,' joked Maggie. 'Leave Aisling with us, love' she added.

Sean gave Cait and me a lift up to the house. He said he had to check his emails but we all knew he'd been waiting for an excuse to leave the bale stacking to the others. Cait and I went straight to YouTube, where there was a film of Cait's latest boyfriend and his mates surfing the big wave down in County Clare.

'What the fuuuuuck!' was Cait's eloquent comment as a friend of theirs from Sligo did a life-threatening ride. We watched agog as a tiny figure surfed inside the tube of a breaking crest, running across the wave's face just ahead of a cascading maelstrom of foam.

'Calm down,' I said. 'He must be alive or he couldn't have texted you to tell you about it.'

'Oh yeah, course, sorry, but Jesus, look at that.'

Sean joined us. He was scowling at his phone. 'Holy fuck, the bastard, I'll kill him.'

'What's up, Sean?' I asked.

'He's not coming, he's stuck in Iceland and wants me to phone him.'

I was sorry. I knew how much Sean had been looking forward to Trigve coming back and to be honest I was, too. He always brought so much fun with him and Aisling simply adored him. Cait and I left him to his phone call while we went down to the kitchen.

After dinner that evening Sean said he'd something to say.

'Some of our original juvenile gannets have been picked up in Iceland, of all places. Trigve's there monitoring herring stocks and he wants me to join him. I could do with some help and I was wondering if there's any chance you could come with me, Clare? We won't be gone long, probably be back by the weekend.'

'Wow, could I?' I looked at Mum and Dad. 'I'd need someone to look after the centre, we've that school booking and … No, I don't think I'll be able to. What about Aisling?'

'We'll take her love, go on, you could do with a break from all this.'

Mum smiled at Aisling, who looked unhappy at the idea, probably because Sean was going away as much as anything.

Sean surprised me when he said, 'Bring her along! Sure, it'd be grand, we won't be working all the time. It's a great place, Iceland. Swimming is the thing there. Even villages have swimming pools, Aisling. It's the geothermal energy,' he added, looking at Dad. 'Free warm water everywhere.'

'Yeah, yeah, please Mammy, I'll be really, really good. Please, please.' She'd seen my doubtful expression and was determined to have it her way.

I would have loved a little break from motherhood but she had a very persuasive personality.

'Really? Brilliant, wow! But what about money, the flights …'

'It's work, love,' Sean said with a wink. 'We'll put Aisling down as a necessary expense.'

But then Dad pointed out that my passport was probably out of date and Aisling didn't even have one.

'Never fear,' Sean reassured. 'I'll book the flights from Dublin and we'll all go up to Nuala's tomorrow to get the passports sorted out. It may take a day or so but where there's a will there's a way.'

# 51: THE NORTH ATLANTIC DRIFT

Sean lifted Aisling into his arms and allowed me to board the aircraft ahead of him. I took the window seat, having promised Aisling that we'd swap places as soon as there was anything to see. As the plane left Dublin on course for Reykjavik, I showed her the book on Iceland I'd bought.

Who'd have guessed I'd be flying over the North Atlantic to a land that seemed a place out of myth, a trinket in the shipping report, an embellishment of the real news about seas closer to home.

'Look, Aisling,' I said. 'It says the sheep here are the biggest in Europe with the longest wool to keep out the cold. We'll have to tell Maggie about them.'

Aisling studied the pictures in the book and then, bored, begged me to let her see out of the window.

'Oh, go on then, I thought you'd rather sit next to Sean.'

We swapped places, which turned out to be a good idea, because within minutes I felt her little body slump next to mine as she slept off all the excitement of the morning.

I turned to Sean, who'd seemed unusually pre-occupied and quiet. I wondered if he was worried about Trigve. Were things cooling off between them?

'Are you okay? You seem quiet,' I said.

He looked at Aisling. 'Is she asleep, Clare?'

I nodded and gave him my best 'you can tell me anything' face.

'Have you ever heard your dad and I talking about the North Atlantic Drift?' he said.

I looked at him blankly.

'You must know what I mean, Clare? The Gulf Stream?' he elucidated.

'Oh yeah, of course, brings warm currents up from the Caribbean and gives us our mild climate.' I braced myself for a lecture about climate change.

'Where do you think it goes after it leaves Irish waters?' he went on.

'Oh, I suppose, um, western Scotland, the Shetlands, the Faeroes. Oh and Norway of course. Ah, maybe this was about Trigve after all.

'As well as Norway it hits the east coast of Iceland, Clare.'

Ok, maybe it wasn't about Trigve after all.

'Clare,' he went on in a teacher's voice. 'If you were to put a message-in-a-bottle into the sea on Carrig na Ron, where would it end up? Don't say America.'

This was fun, a geography quiz from my favourite lecturer.

'Ah ha, this is about how our gannets have ended up in Iceland, isn't it?' I answered feeling pleased with myself.

'Yes and no, love.' He took my hand and looking very concerned, double checked that Aisling still slept and then he asked me: 'What do you think might happen if you dropped a currach into the sea off Carrig na Ron. If the currach had a sail and the skipper was unconscious?'

My heart dropped to my bowels as the truth I'd always known became plain. They must have found the wreck, or his body. He squeezed my hand as I turned and stared out of the window. I couldn't look at him. Here it was at last. My closure. The closure I'd always needed or so I thought. Until this moment there'd always been that miniscule chance that he was still alive. Now it was over.

'Clare, love. There's more. Trigve asked me to bring you because he thought it only fair that you see him first.'

I was shocked at the pointlessness of that. 'But isn't his body all rotted away by now? Why would I want to see that?' My lip began to quiver and hot tears poured unbidden down my face. I thought I'd done my grieving but obviously there was still an endless well of un-cried tears.

'No love, you don't understand. He isn't dead, Clare. He's alive and apparently he lives in Iceland.'

# 52: ICELAND

We left Reykjavik in a propeller plane that took us to the little airport of Egilsstadir in eastern Iceland. It was hard to imagine that it was midsummer and that the sun would never set. Aisling jabbered away to Sean in the two seats in front of me and I looked out at the land below. The plane flew under the clouds and I saw Iceland's interior in detail. No roads or towns to see, simply mountains, mountains and more mountains, blue-green glaciers and a lumpy white duvet of snow reaching to the horizon. It surprised me to see so much snow in the middle of June and I wondered how much more there could be in winter. What could Ronan be doing here? My mind went over it a hundred times, how would he have travelled and how long did it take? And the biggest question of all: why hadn't he come home? It went round and round in my head.

Sean had told me that he and Trigve thought that it might only have taken Ronan three days, if the boat had picked up a good current. I could hardly bear to think about him in the currach with no protection from the winds and waves, and ocean-going ships.

'Ronan must have had an angel with him, Clare,' he said for the umpteenth time.

The mystery of his journey was one thing. What I couldn't get my head around was the fact that in five whole years he hadn't so much as sent a postcard. Why hadn't he at least come home to put his poor father out of his misery? The answer was that it couldn't be true, and that Trigve had imagined the likeness of Ronan to some other man.

'What about Donal, Sean? Have you told him?'

'No, love. Um, to be honest I didn't want to put him through it, until I knew definitively. I mean, I am sure what Trigve says is right,' he said, taking in my shocked expression. 'But I need to be absolutely certain. Anyway, he'd probably think it was just a crazy notion of Trigve's. We'll phone him tonight.'

The plane landed with a series of bumps and a screech of brakes. We walked down the steps into a parched, brown landscape. A fierce northerly wind nearly blew us over. I looked around for Trigve's familiar face and jumped when two big arms, encircling from behind, picked me right off my feet.

'Ha, here you are. Welcome to the land of fire and ice.' Trigve dropped me and turned to Sean who he kissed on the mouth without a care. Sean pulled away.

'It's ok; you're in Iceland now, where nobody cares about things like that.

Come on, I have things to tell you,' he added.

I let Trigve take our bags and followed him out to a waiting hire-car.

'We have to make a journey to Eskifjordur,' he said.

The scenery really was spectacular. Huge mountains gave way to sheets of lava and at several points on the journey Trigve pointed out bubbling mud pools. The air reeked of rotten eggs, which Trigve explained was normal in areas of volcanic activity. I was only half listening. All I could think about was Ronan. I kept expecting him to pop up in front of me and felt both relieved and disappointed when he didn't.

'I will take you to the gannets later but first we have a treat.' Trigve wanted to surprise us and wouldn't tell us what it was until we got there. I wondered what was going on. Never mind the gannet colony, where was Ronan?

Aisling was delighted when Trigve led us into what looked like a swimming pool complex. We showered and walked out through the changing room doors. Instead of a pool, there lay a steaming lake. The water seemed to stretch on forever as the steam prevented us from seeing its edges. Vague shapes of people appeared and vanished in the sulphurous fog, they swam or simply stood in the swirling waters. We followed Trigve in, amazed at the warmth of the water.

'It's a natural hot spring, you like it, I hope?' Trigve looked at us with a beaming grin. 'I'm taking Clare to the mud pool, Sean, you swim with

Aisling,' he pulled me away and I gratefully followed him, at last he might tell me something concrete about Ronan. He showed me how to take mud from the bottom and rub it into my skin and hair. It was slimy and smelly but he assured me I'd feel wonderful afterwards. As we wallowed in the shallows he told me a story. The story was called Petur Peturson.

# 53: PETUR PETURSON

Petur Peturson was a carpenter. He was the son of a carpenter called Petur Peturson and his grandfather was also called Petur.

The family trade was boat building and they all made a reasonable living building and repairing boats in the eastern Icelandic port of Eskifjordur. The men of the family were very large and although Petur Peturson had tasted whale meat, he grew up on a diet of herring and fly-caught local salmon from some of the finest salmon rivers in the world.

Petur's wife lived out on a spit of land at the end of the fjord. Her family had cattle and sheep and when he married her, he moved into the farm with them. He loved to sit at their big wooden table eating the mutton stew that was their staple food. Every morning and evening he cycled thirteen kilometres along the coast road that runs between the boat yards of Eskifjordur and the farm.

On a fine late summer evening, five years ago, something caught Petur's eye as he cycled home. It appeared to be a skipper-less boat, and though he was an expert on all types of craft he had never seen one like this before. He waved and shouted and, failing to catch the attention of anyone on board, he went back along the coast hoping that the little boat would be pushed ashore by the currents onto a shingle spit where driftwood tended to collect.

It did indeed drive ashore and Petur waded into the water to pull it to safety. In a flash he took in all the details of its marvellous construction. A light wooden frame covered in black-tarred canvas. A lugsail, now torn but still standing, was attached to the bow. It had obviously been designed to give the boat speed, perhaps for racing. Petur had heard that boats like this had once come from southern Atlantic islands. But he had never seen such a boat. He decided he would take the design and make one for himself. This boat was light enough for one person to carry up a shore and he could imagine himself in it, out fishing for herring on fine summer evenings.

But he couldn't give it much more thought because lying in the boat was a man. He seemed to be dead until, when Petur poked him, the man stirred. What definitely wasn't dead was a black dog that snarled and snapped when he poked the man. Petur cycled away for help and, by evening, the man and dog were sleeping at his wife's farm while Petur drew plans of the boat.

The man recovered from his journey but was unable to tell them who he was or where he'd come from. He spoke a language that nobody understood. His wife and her parents tried to decide what it was. It wasn't Norwegian. It wasn't English. It wasn't French or Italian. It wasn't German or Russian. In the end they thought it must be a made-up language caused by a head injury and they left him in peace. After a week he stopped using the strange language and spoke English to them, which they understood little better.

After two weeks the man was strong enough to get up and Petur invited him to help at the boatyard. He quietly worked away all day on the boats that Petur and his father made. He showed Petur how to tar a canvas currach and they spent many a companionable hour silently fishing from a variety of boats they made together. Petur's sister-in-law set her sights on the handsome stranger but he looked at her sadly seeming only to want his black dog for company. And that's all there was to say about Petur and the man from the sea.

# 54: PIZZA AND TEARS

Dressed and glowing after our natural spa, we got back into Trigve's car and set off for Eskifjordur. The volcanic landscape looked inhospitable and alien. What was Ronan doing in such a stark place? How could he prefer this to the lush country around Carran? Even Seal Island had more trees. All around us, black mountains reared out of the charred land. We passed basalt cliffs and steaming rocks, which did nothing to ease my sense of foreboding and trembling trepidation.

'Trigve's off to find him, Clare,' Sean reassured. 'We'll go, and I thought perhaps some lunch first.' He steered us out of the car park's shadow into the crisp arctic light of eastern Iceland.

Despite my nerves and uncertainty, I was starving. The café was a pizza place with enticing smells of cooked cheese and dough. As we ate, the hollow feeling in my stomach lessened, though every few minutes a spasm of panic and fear made me put down my fork. Aisling chattered away to Sean about aeroplanes and Iceland. I sat in silence, trying to make sense of my feelings.

Since the morning flight from Dublin I'd moved from shock and relief to numb anger. I saw no earthly reason why he hadn't contacted me. At first it felt like rejection, that he hadn't really cared for me after all. Now it felt like cowardice. What kind of man would do that, not only to his lover, but to his father, too? I thought of him as a loser and a freak. But his dark eyes kept swimming into my mind. Five years on I still dreamed of him. We were always on the island, often in the bay, swimming through green water, together. No matter how hard I tried to hate him, there he was: my soul mate.

Sean nudged me. I looked up, but all I saw was a blur as my eyes filled with tears. It was too hard. I really wasn't sure I wanted to see Ronan at all. And

I wished Aisling wasn't there. What on earth would she make of it all? I'd given her a fantasy daddy, telling her about our seals and dreams and the little black boat. I'd tried to make him seem like a very special person, a selkie man who came from the sea and went back to the sea. I didn't want her thinking he was nothing but a coward. But he was. Cait had been right. The memory of the kisses in the cave, that had sustained me for so long, were just salt spray on the wind, of no use to anybody at all.

Sean touched my hand in a gesture of support. At this, my eyes brimmed over.

'I don't want to see him,' I blurted.

Aisling, who'd been minding her own business with a colouring book, looked up sharply.

'My daddy,' she said. 'I'm going to see my daddy, aren't I?' She set her blue eyes in a forceful stare. 'My daddy's a sailor and a fisherman, you know,' she told Sean. 'He builds boats and he sailed across the ocean,' she smiled at us. 'And he can swim like a seal and he's got a dog called Puffin who's an angel, really. Come on, we've got to go and see him.'

She stood and pushed her chair back. I don't know how she knew what we were up to. She always was telepathic with me. But I certainly didn't want to discuss it with her.

'Sean,' I whispered. 'Can you take Aisling for me? If I'm to meet him I think I should be on my own.'

'Mammy, what's the matter,' was Aisling's inevitable response. 'I want to come with you.' She began to cry, too.

Sean looked up at the waitresses who were watching Aisling's mounting wails. He shrugged apologetically and got up to pay the bill. 'I'll try Trigve,' he said over his shoulder and disappeared outside to find a phone signal.

We went to the ladies' and I patted cold water over my eyes. There wasn't much point as the tears kept seeping through. I gave up. Who cared what I looked like? It was too much to ask of a girl that she look good during such an ordeal. When we came out, Trigve had appeared as if by magic. He was talking urgently to Sean who looked concerned and glanced through the window as he listened. He caught my eye through the glass and smiled his usual optimistic grin at us.

Sean swept Aisling up into his arms. 'Come on, I've a surprise for you,' he said.

'I'm going to meet my daddy, he's a sailor and a ...'

He interrupted her. 'I've a group of seals to show you first.' That seemed to satisfy her. 'And they might not be there if we don't hurry.' Trigve nodded at Sean who walked off with Aisling on his shoulders, her dark plaits bouncing as they went.

# 55: HIS HANDS

'You should have been here last week,' Trigve chatted as we walked along the dockside. 'We had a pair of blue whales at the end of the fjord.' He smiled at me, waiting for an enthusiastic response. None came.

'Hey, don't cry,' he said, putting his arm around me.

'I don't know why I can't stop,' I sniffed, and continued. 'I didn't think I'd ever see him again. I didn't know I still felt like this.' My mouth was dry and an ache pressured my sternum.

We walked arm in arm along a wooden pontoon and he began climbing down onto a trawler.

'The other way's blocked and this cuts off having to walk round by the road.' He held his hand out for me and guided me up and down the gangways and decks of Eskifjordur's off-duty herring fleet. When we reached the far side of the docks, I looked around expecting to see Ronan. There was nobody there, just an old man standing by a bench having a smoke. I clutched Trigve's arm and stared. On the ground next to the white-haired man was a familiar black dog.

Puffin ran over barking and the man called him off. I very nearly fainted when it hit me. His hair was long and had turned completely white. He'd grown a beard and his face was lined and so thin. I felt sick and leaned against Trigve, who let go of my hand and pushed me towards him. We stood six feet apart and stared at each other. We stared and stared and neither of us spoke. Then I thought my knees would give way and I staggered to the bench.

He sat next to me and after an age he took my hand. At first I wanted to pull it away but when I looked down I realised that I'd never forgotten that hand. Every vein and bump was familiar to me and not only that. He had the same hands as Aisling. Even the shape of the nails was the same. I pulled his hand to my mouth and breathed it in. I didn't say anything; there was nothing to say. I waited for him to speak and eventually he did.

'I had a boat full of herring, you know. I was on my way back against the squall. I lost control of the sail and the mast cracked my head. When I woke it was dark and I'd no idea where I was. The sail had torn, right down the middle into two ragged pieces. I'd no choice but to let the current take her. The Atlantic Drift dropped the currach on a shingle shore and I was nearly dead from thirst when Petur found me. He said I spoke only in Irish for a week or so, but I don't remember that.'

'But you didn't contact me. Your dad! Why? Why didn't you tell us?' My voice croaked from all the crying and adrenaline. I felt dreamy, floating and unreal. I didn't even feel anger at that point.

He took his hand from me and stroked my face. 'There's something I've been thinking about these last five years,' he said. 'I can't use it as an excuse, but maybe it'll help you understand.' He stooped over and I saw the familiar line of his neck. He took hold of my hand again. 'After I got here ... I had a kind of breakdown, I suppose. I'd been thinking that things with you would be over when the summer ended. You wanted to travel or go off to university and your father, and mine and Bridie, as well, had all warned me not to stand in your way. Anyway I knew that deep down we wanted different things.

Everybody, even my father, told me to forget you. Then there was the island. Sean insisted I'd never be allowed to live there properly once the place was a sanctuary.

I never intended to leave and I'd certainly never dreamed of going to Iceland, hardly knew it existed. But the gods took me and it seemed the perfect answer. I did have herring for you that day and all I could think of was hauling the currach up onto the beach and you'd be waiting there for me. But then when the sea took me, I knew in my heart that it was my mother calling me back.'

'Your mother? ... But surely after a few weeks you must have known we'd be looking for you.'

'The weeks went by and it was easy, living with Petur, building boats. A simple and fulfilling life for a person like me. It was easy not to think too much about anything. And then there's something I've come to understand in my years here,' he said. I opened my mouth to protest but he carried on.

'When my mother drowned I was on the boat with her. My mother had turned her back on the island. She hated to be reminded of what was lost. She never came out on the boat. Partly because there's a feeling amongst fishermen that women bring bad luck to fishing boats, partly because she couldn't bring herself to go back to the island. It was my seventh birthday. I didn't understand my mother and I begged her to come with us. I loved her and wanted her with me all the time. I thought we could all have a grand day out with a picnic and ... I begged her to come with us, Clare.

I was desperate to show her what a great little sailor I'd become. We came back without her. It was *my* fault she drowned and I've *always* known that. If I hadn't begged her to come ... What's more, my father blamed me too. He never spoke about her death but I saw him looking at me and I saw accusation in his eyes.

I have no doubt that he's not been sorry to see the back of me, the son who caused his mother's death.'

'How can you say that?' I protested.

'I was in the skipper's chair pretending to be the captain of the boat, feeling so grown up. My father went out to call her in out of the wind. She was standing at the bows one minute and then he couldn't find her and, well, you know the rest.' He stopped talking and turned to me. 'Can you see now, Clare, why I'm so messed up?'

I felt anger at his stupidity, but sadness for the pain I could feel in him. 'You know it wasn't your fault, don't you,' I said. 'Your dad never blamed you. You were a child. A boy. You should have seen him. He's been desperate, how could you not know how loved you are? By him and me and Bridie and everybody.' I wanted to hit him and hug him at the same time. I could see him as a little boy, not much older than Aisling. 'Ronan, I've missed you so much, please come home to me.'

'Trigve told me I was an idiot to blame myself and I can see that now. He also told me about Aisling. You know, I'd have come back if I'd known you were pregnant. I've thought of you everyday, imagining you away working on a project in Africa or living in Cork having a great life with new friends.'

He paused and looked at me. 'I don't suppose I've any right to meet her?'

'She thinks her daddy's got dark hair so she might not believe it's you.' I stroked his hair. It was thick and quite suited him but it would take some getting used to. The Ronan of my dreams still had black hair. The beard needed a serious trim.

'My hair went like this within months of my coming here, part of the breakdown, I suppose.' He stroked my face. 'You've not changed at all. Still my beautiful, green-eyed Clare.' He pulled me close and began kissing me and if Trigve hadn't interrupted us, we'd probably never have stopped.

Aisling sat on a grassy bank with Sean. She saw me and ran over.

'Mammy! Mammy, come and see the seals! There's one staring at me. I think it's the one from the island.' She pulled my hand, oblivious to the tall stranger behind her. She must have forgotten all about the premonition of her sailor-daddy.

Ronan laughed for the first time since our meeting and as I turned to him he whispered into my ear. 'I can hardly believe it. She's gorgeous, Clare. So like you in every way but for one thing. She has my mother's eyes.'

# 56: THE SEALS OF CARRIG NA RON

*Saoirse* rode the swell with ease. It was my first time out to the island with Ronan since his return, and my feelings about it were as turbulent as the waves beneath us. He sat in the skipper's chair looking straight ahead, with a frown flickering on and off his forehead. We'd brought food and bedding and a bale of turf for the fire. It was to be our first night on the island in five years.

'Carrig na Ron hasn't changed a bit, since you were here,' Donal put his hand on Ronan's shoulder and looked helplessly towards me. Ronan didn't respond.

I could see a muscle in his jaw moving rhythmically and knew he was grinding his teeth. He'd been doing it in his sleep since Iceland, and sometimes it was loud enough to wake me up.

Sean came to the rescue with a monologue about the gannets directed at Ronan. 'Our gannet colony is growing and our great news is that the fledglings from our first brood are rearing their own chicks. They're fledged themselves now and ready to go.'

'Where do they go?' Donal asked. Ronan continued staring ahead.

'Ah well, it's very interesting,' Sean continued. 'They all go south to the African coast for starters, but nobody can say where they'll end up. Some will go to Scotland, some to Norway, the odd one might end up in Iceland.' He laughed at that, and Ronan flicked a look towards him. 'But most will come back here, to where they were born. That's the way it is with gannets.'

'Is that so, Sean?' Donal looked at his son as he spoke. 'Ronan, will I bring *Saoirse* in or will you do it yourself?'

'I'll do it.'

The tide was well out as we landed and Ronan had to manoeuvre *Saoirse* into a gap between the quay and the rocks on the other side where the water was deeper.

'Grand job,' Donal said. 'I'll wait for you, Sean. I've a couple of repairs to get on with while you're gone.'

'Ok, Donal, I won't be long. But why don't you come and see them for yourself? You've never been up to the stacks.'

Donal looked from Sean to Ronan. Ronan's spell seemed to have broken. He smiled at his father and said he'd like Donal to see the gannets. I hung back with Sean and left Donal to walk the hill path with Ronan. I could see Ronan gesticulating with his arms, explaining the position of the colony perhaps. I smiled at Sean. He put his arm around my shoulder.

'It'll take time, love. He has a way to go. Whatever he felt about his mother, his past, his father, then and now, it's all going to take time. You and Aisling are the best things for him. He can't stay in his bubble for long with her around.' He smiled and squeezed my arm. 'And I'd say he's already on the mend. Look!'

I could see that Sean was right. The two of them had climbed up onto the highest point above the stacks, where they turned back to look down at us. They were both laughing.

By the time Sean and I arrived gasping beside them, Ronan had pointed out all the wonders of our gannets to his father. We all sat together watching them fishing, and we counted chicks, and the empty nests where youngsters had fledged and flown. And then it was time for Sean and Donal to leave and we were left alone, at last, on our island.

The black beach seemed to be steaming in the afternoon sun. A shimmering heat haze made it look more like a mirage than solid rock, enhancing the dreamlike state I'd been in since arriving on the island. I clutched his arm as we walked down the steep path onto the beach.

I'd been expecting him to enter some weird catharsis on the island. To grow distant and aloof, as he so often used to do. But he didn't. He pulled me to the mouth of our cave and turned me to face him.

'Listen, I need to tell you, not a day went by that I didn't dream of you. You became my imaginary friend. On the one hand I thought of you away travelling. But then there was another you that lived in my dreams, in my soul. Your dark hair and your green eyes coloured every thought, everything I did.

While I worked on Petur's boats I imagined taking you out in them. When I walked the coast road, I imagined you arm in arm with me. And when I lay down to sleep, I put my pillow sideways so that I could pretend it was you in my arms. And … ' He paused and a tear fell from his eye and ran down to his chin. I'd never seen him cry before. 'I'm sorry,' he said, and then he collapsed into my arms and sobbed and sobbed like a child.

'Oh, my love,' I whispered over and over again.

'Why didn't I call you?' he muttered. 'Where was my head, for so long? I might never have found you, or Aisling.' He stood back and stared at me. 'Can you ever forgive me? Can you really have me back after what I've done?'

'I love you,' I told him. 'It's all that matters. You are mine and I'm yours.'

We kissed the tears from each other's faces and held each other until the sun began to sink. And then, at last, we made love on the warm black rock, and I thought my heart would burst, to have him back with me again. Afterwards, I rolled away from him as something caught the corner of my eye.

'Hey,' I whispered. 'Look over there.'

'They've come to welcome us home.'

While we'd been in our lovers' cocoon, a dozen or more seals had hauled up the beach behind us. Moving very slowly, we positioned ourselves and sat watching while they lay crooning and preening, until their fur began to dry. The females looked very sleek and fat. Ronan whispered that they'd soon be having their pups.

'We could make a hide here, you know. And watch the babies grow.' He hugged me to him.

I smiled at the thought of that.

'And we'll bring Aisling. We can make her a little bed in the nook beside the fire.' He grinned at me.

I'd never seen his face look so open and genuinely happy. Snuggling into his arms, I sighed a long sigh of relief and contentment.

'I love you,' I said.

'I love you more,' he replied.

Ronan has made another currach that he's called Aisling. Of course I never want him to go fishing alone, but my wild island man cannot be completely tamed, even by a love as strong as ours. All I can do is pray that when he goes out to sea the seals and the gannets of Carrig na Ron will guide him safely home to me.

# ACKNOWLEDGEMENTS

Sue and Geoff and Dolphinwatch Carrigaholt. Richard Williams for believing in me as a writer. Tom Griffiths for your vision and beautiful photography. All my writing buddies: Anthony Ferner, Sally Tissington, and Mez Packer for the invaluable sessions in our cottage in Wales. All the folk who kindly read my work with special thanks to Mandy, Ella Guthrie and Louise. Jamie Wilson and Pete Woodbridge for work on the cover design. Dave Steele Mac services. Jake Mac Siacais for Irish translation. Brie Burkeman my ever supportive and patient agent and her assistant, Marlee Newman for editorial help. Didi my sea swim buddy. Mum and Dad who gave me my passion for Ireland. And...my selkie.